T0101938

Out of the Sugar Factory

Out of the Sugar Factory

Dorothee Elmiger

Translated from Swiss German by
Megan Ewing

TWO LINES
PRESS

Originally published as *Aus der Zuckerfabrik*
Copyright © 2020 by Carl Hanser Verlag GmbH & Co. KG, München
Translation copyright © 2023 by Megan Ewing

Two Lines Press
582 Market Street, Suite 700, San Francisco, CA 94104
www.twolinespress.com

ISBN: 978-1-949641-40-0
Ebook ISBN: 978-1-949641-41-7

Cover design by Najeebah Al-Ghadban
Interior Design by Sloane | Samuel
Printed in the United States of America

Library of Congress Cataloging-in-Publication Data:
Names: Elmiger, Dorothee, 1985- author. | Ewing, Megan, translator.
Title: Out of the sugar factory / Dorothee Elmiger;
translated by Megan Ewing.
Other titles: Aus der Zuckerfabrik. English
Identifiers: LCCN 2022047081 (print) | LCCN 2022047082 (ebook) | ISBN
9781949641400 (paperback) | ISBN 9781949641417 (ebook)
Subjects: LCGFT: Novels.
Classification: LCC PT2705.L65 A9613 2023 (print) | LCC PT2705.L65
(ebook) | DDC 833/.92--dc23/eng/20221007
LC record available at https://lccn.loc.gov/2022047081
LC ebook record available at https://lccn.loc.gov/2022047082

1 3 5 7 9 10 8 6 4 2

This book is supported in part by an award from the
National Endowment for the Arts,
and with the support of the Swiss Arts Council Pro Helvetia.

NATIONAL
ENDOWMENT for the ARTS
arts.gov

swiss arts council
prohelvetia

For J.

Body my house
my horse my hound
what will I do
when you are fallen

Where will I sleep
How will I ride
What will I hunt

—May Swenson, from "Question"

Wo ist Zucker, ich find's nicht
Zucker!
—Wolfram Lotz, *Heilige Schrift I*

– It's like this: I'm walking through brambles, through undergrowth. And some birds are chirping too.

– And then?

– Nothing else, it just goes on and on like that.

– But you like it, the brambles.

– What else should I say about it?

– Whether you like it, these brambles, you can say that; what you want from it; what's in it for you.

– But I'm in the middle of it. You obviously have no sense of what it's like in there.

– I imagine it's very messy, without order or definition. And beautiful because most anything could happen in there and because, depending on the time of day, the light falls one place then another, and sometimes there's snow. And it's also annoying because you're constantly getting caught on the branches in the undergrowth, especially if they have thorns, and you do so enjoy wearing those velvet pants.

– All right already.

– So then do you walk around or what? What do you do in there?

– Nothing, nothing at all. I maybe go a few steps, and then sometimes I stop and smoke a cigarette.

– And the birds?

– Yes, them I like.

Plaisir

The sun is always shining when I wake up now.

On TV, a documentary about a pineapple farm near Santo Domingo. Wide, white-clouded sky. Haitian workers in the fields throw the ripe fruit to each other.

Then the *Pineapple King* enters the picture; he stands in the field and talks to the camera. Before he bought these 180 hectares in the '80s, he was a vegetable farmer in the Zurich lowlands.

The sembradores put seedlings in the soil without pausing.

The *Pineapple King* measures the sugar content of his fruit for TV.

Later he pays out wages.

A worker's T-shirt: MY SKILLS NEVER END

—

A second film: Karl Feierabend, a distiller from Rotkreuz who emigrated to the tropics to become a large-scale farmer. He drives four geese over the green landscape with his horse. Grasses, meadows, palm trees. The sky, completely colorless.

—

A message from France: This winter, I am to speak at a school in a Paris suburb about my work. The principal, I'm told, wants to pick me up in a car from the Latin Quarter and drive me to Plaisir where the Collège Guillaume Apollinaire is located, and then bring me back to the hotel.

—

Makeshift explanations when someone asks what I'm working on.
    A Philadelphia parking lot (NEW WORLD PLAZA)
    Desire
    Sugar, LOTTO, *Overseas*

Annette at dinner: Two years ago, she said, she read a novel by an Australian writer in which a long series of abruptly appearing images was described; each image evoked the next, which is to say they were, at minimum, loosely connected and thus formed a kind of path—a luminous path, she claimed, through the things.

When I leaf through my notebooks and photocopies, the illustrations, diagrams, and photographs, when I open the files created over the course of the past months, I see no path—no images or illuminations overlapping each other at the edges, pointing to each other—but instead a place, a point from which I started four or five years ago. Since then, everything I've touched, everything I've seen that seemed connected with the first location, I've carried it back and set it down in that encompassing space.

Like the yew trees from the Plaisir castle grounds, which are shaped like sugarloaves. The shopping center in the northern part of the city (GRAND PLAISIR), La Mosquée de Plaisir.

There is no fixed order to this place: with each stride through the chaos—across the pineapple fields of Monte Plata, through the Parisian suburbs or the long-abandoned garden of a sanatorium, over the Sicilian mountains, past the Russian baths of Philadelphia, to the banks of the Swan River in Australia—objects seem to enter into new relationships, new constellations with each other.

—

Through the landscapes, this experimental configuration of things, this *essai*, I return again and again to one scene; the first time I saw it, something seemed to reveal itself to me that I couldn't articulate but could only rediscover in circumstances of similar or analogous structure—as relationships, repetitions, parallels.

1986: Men stand tightly packed in the low hall of an inn in Spiez on the southern shore of the Thunersee, between them are their sons—boys of twelve, thirteen—and some women, wives, mothers. Warm light illuminates the assembled citizenry of the village, who spill out into the hallway. They all ultimately turn to one man, as if to the preacher of a profane mass. In his hands, he holds out two figures above the heads of the assembly, two female figures made of wood or polished black stone, maybe thirty centimeters high. The bodies, gleaming in the light, are unclothed except for some fabric wound loosely around their waists and heads, and gold necklaces. They kneel in seeming self-absorption. Then the auctioneer raises his voice: *Who's bidding? I need silence, Twenty twenty francs A fiver Twenty-five Another bid Just look at these breasts Thirty-five Who can go a little higher Thirty-five francs is the bid Thirty-five francs going once going twice three times and these old N—— are sold*

The more I return to this room, which I know only from a documentary produced in the '80s, the clearer it becomes that my urge to revisit this place has nothing to do with the chance that something might reveal itself with any particular clarity to me. On the contrary, I now suspect that these recurrent visits, my neurotic pilgrimages, are grounded in the fact that the scene is, so to speak, *irresolvable*: a brief convergence of the most diverse strands of history—as if disparate rocky objects, celestial bodies that had long been circling the sun, seemingly unconnected, suddenly collided, and their impact provided an illumination of things, of rubble and dust, one second long.

—

A stanza from John Berryman's *Dream Song 311*: "Hunger was constitutional with him, / women, cigarettes, liquor, need need need / until he went to pieces. / The pieces sat up & wrote. They did not heed / their piecedom but kept very quietly on / among the chaos."

When I linger on this strange colonization, in these geographical patches with their associated testimonies, artifacts, and phantasms, what I'm up to seems to deal with *hunger as constitution*, with the "urge," as Ortega y Gasset puts it, "to get out of oneself" that underlies everything orgiastic ("drunkenness, mysticism, infatuation, etc."). Perhaps it would be correct to say that this hunger is the real object of my research, the place where the Haitian worker (MY SKILLS NEVER END) sleeps in the shade of the trees in the Plaisir castle gardens, etc., and at the same time hunger is the reason *for* my research, the driving force of this little production.

—

Riding the last train home between the mountains of the Upper Valais. The snow-covered mountainsides are bright in the night, above them the dark, high peaks against a deep blue sky. Spiez, Thun, Bern. I fall asleep on the way, dream I published a volume titled *The Lyrical Moderation of Immoderateness*.

—

Watched Chantal Akerman's "J'ai faim, j'ai froid" (1984) again. *Éducation sentimentale* of the young woman in ten minutes. The two seventeen-year-olds have good haircuts. They walk through the French capital hungry, their appetites immense and encompassing all, I think, things and people and landscapes.

They gaze into the displays of snack bars and stores, through the windows into the interior of the illuminated eateries. They're hungry not because they haven't eaten in a long time, but because eating gives them such delirious pleasure.

– *J'ai faim.* [I'm hungry.]
– *Viens.* [Come.]
– *Combien il reste d'argent?* [How much money is left?]
– *Rien.* [None.]
– *Bon, c'est maintenant que la vie commence.* [Good, now life begins.]
– *Qu'est-ce qu'on fait?* [What are we going to do?]
– *On cherche du travail.* [We find work.]
– *Bon. Où c'est qu'on va?* [Okay, where do you want to go?]
– *Je ne sais pas.* [I don't know.]
– *Qu'est-ce que tu sais faire, toi?* [What do you know how to do?]
– *Je sais coudre, écrire, compter, lire, chanter.* [I can sew, write, count, read, and sing.]
– *Moi aussi, mais j'aime pas coudre, écrire, compter, lire. J'aime que chanter.* [Me too, but I don't like to sew, write, count, or read. I only like to sing.]
– *Moi, je chante faux et je crie quand je chante.* [When I sing I scream out of tune.]
– *Moi, j'aime crier, je chante juste.* [I like screaming,

I sing fine.]
– *On va chanter alors*. [Let's sing then.]

How the two of them enter a restaurant afterward and start singing, not really knowing how the melody goes; how they stand between the tables with mouths wide, awkward and out of place and beautiful. And how slender their necks are.

That's pretty much what I'm attempting to do here too, at least as far as I've always imagined it.

One of the last scenes: While one of them is lying in bed with a man
("*J'ai envie de t'aimer.*" "*Aime-moi, alors.*") [I want to love you." "Then love me."]
the other cracks eggs on the edge of the pan in his kitchen.

—

C., as we walk past the gymnasium: He rarely experiences hunger; in fact, the feeling of hunger has always been quite foreign to him.

How he strides across the wide meadows of the former military training grounds, so pale and tall in his coat, as if he's from an impoverished family of aristocrats.

In my case, on the other hand, every sentence I write lately means:
J'ai faim. / Aime-moi, alors.

But for weeks all my offerings have been politely rejected by the man with no appetite,

even the fruit I'm always careful to polish with a handkerchief before offering to him.

We walk through open country, golden fields, by ponds. At some point we cross the highway. Far below us tiny vehicles shoot along the road into the end of the workday.

—

In the mail, a book from S., a collection of "Biographies of the Insane" from the late eighteenth century. He thought—he writes—the texts might be of interest to me.

The Hospital for the Insane at P.

The love-mad Jakob W***r, who believes he has a glass chest and thus a heart that anyone and everyone can see.

The young woman from B.—abandoned by a man, tall "like a poplar on a swollen river"—who is always climbing up into the crowns of trees.

When she falls from the roof of her parents' house and dies, the townspeople trail the coffin through the city streets, the priest declaiming: 𝕳𝖊 𝖑𝖊𝖋𝖙 𝖒𝖊, 𝖇𝖚𝖙 𝖙𝖍𝖊 𝕷𝖔𝖗𝖉 𝖙𝖔𝖔𝖐 𝖒𝖊 𝖚𝖕!

—

Heading home around two o'clock in the morning across the meadows in the park, the dry stalks break, crackling under my shoes.

—

I know—I write to C.—I know a foreign place, a tropical place where partridges wander through shady groves, red-eyed turtles lie motionless in stagnant water, silver doves nest in the crowns of tall trees... And as I write, a universal chirping of birds begins outside.

—

Dream: After midnight I wake up and go downstairs. I know I am in my parents' house. From the hallway I see the light still on in the kitchen, which doesn't surprise me because my mother, an elementary school teacher, spent many nights of my childhood bent over the kitchen table. To her right, the just-graded notebooks; to her left, the stack still to be corrected. In my adolescence, too, she would sit there under the low-hanging lamp, often still at work when I came home late on the last train.

Now as I approach the kitchen, I see that my mother is not holding a pencil but a spindle in her hand—a spindle, I recall instantly, I had seen lying around on the second floor of my grandmother's house amid the wintering plants, old dolls, and Dürrenmatt's *Die Panne* just a few weeks before she, my mother's mother, died. I must have passed it countless times during my visits over the years, but never paid much attention to it: it seemed to have gone unused for a long time.

Just before the light streaming through the kitchen door into the hallway catches me, I stop. I'm wearing a white T-shirt with the words "International Institute for Sport" that reaches almost to my knees. I am maybe eleven years old.

My mother, who seems to be giving her full attention to this spindle, hasn't noticed me yet. I watch her as she deftly handles the device with extraordinary speed. She uses the spindle as if an unknown spirit has entered her or a long-forgotten knowledge has been restored, and as she does, her face changes; new features superimpose on the old ones, or earlier features reemerge beneath the familiar shape of her face.

I'm still standing in the dark, embarrassed to be witnessing the transformation, these states of my mother, the meaning of which I do not know. I enter the kitchen and snatch the thing from her hand, and at that moment it happens that I jab myself with it—I ram the tip of the stupid spindle deep under the skin of my left index finger. Blood drips on my T-shirt and I think, *oh no, not the left hand*, since I'm left-handed.

Carrying the hand in front of me as if it weren't mine, I climb the stairs again and lie down on my childhood bed. I spend weeks and months, eventually years in a state of lethargy. Often, I barely stir over the course of a day. Occasionally I go downstairs to the kitchen and let a few handfuls of Kellogg's Corn Flakes trickle into my mouth, then I go lie back down.

When my mother goes to the movies to see *Independence Day*, to watch the film for the second time, I go along, seeing with my own adolescent eyes how the great alien discs decouple from the mothership and slowly slide in front of the sun.

Bellevue

I enter the place where I've temporarily stored things, this hypothetical attic, just as I have sometimes gone into Italian churches and chapels at midday to escape the heat: brief rounds, a quick stroll in semi-darkness along the opulent side aisles of which no one seems to take notice.

Running my hands over the surfaces, touching everything.

To Laura in the cafeteria: Truthfully, right now I'm just sitting there and reading.

—

In Marie Luise Kaschnitz's last writings, titled *Places*, the description of herself dancing with the patients of a "genteel lunatic asylum" on Lake Constance that she does not name; then her memory of a child, the son of the director of the asylum: In the sanatorium garden at night, he "approached a thick tree with two lighted candles and held those little flames to the bark, convinced that he would succeed in making the mighty tree catch fire." That same night, fireworks rise into the air: "Plants made of light," Kaschnitz writes, and good cheer, in the windows are the applauding patients.

For days now, I've been imagining this boy—sleep-walking, ghostlike almost—moving through the dark garden, flickering candles in his hands; every so often the fireworks exploding above him illuminate the scenery and his face. As if following an intuition, an invitation for him alone, he seeks out the tree and tries to set it alight, to make it go up in flames, to transform it into a glowing sign in the sanatorium garden.

The split-second illumination in the text as a bookmark. Just as Hermann Burger's glass suddenly begins to tremble as he passes Badgastein in the dining car: "as if a medium were trying to communicate with me."

He says he knew "that something was up, but not what."

—

How often I have thrown open Kaschnitz's notes to a random page or read them over from the beginning—the first page, where she, Kaschnitz, writes that this is what has occurred to her in the last few years but "not in sequence," i.e., unordered, and the second page, whose opening lines I can practically recite by heart: *Or places never seen, Stockholm for instance, or Aden on the Red Sea, or Samarkand* and so forth,
    the images of oil towers, oil ships, the great heat in Aden,
    the alien ships, the pleasure ships, all pass by.

And then all of a sudden the sanatorium on page 64, which I immediately recognize: one winter, three or four years ago, I would occasionally pass the voluptuous grounds, and even earlier as a child I sometimes went swimming nearby with my aunt in a small, shady cove.

—

To start with this passage, in this garden: It was as if I had been sitting indecisively on the fence of a paddock for a long time, going back and forth about how a horse, an animal weighing maybe five or six hundred kilos, could best be bridled; finally, annoyed by my own dithering, I threw myself unceremoniously onto one of them, holding on as tightly as I possibly could.

The matter of the bridle I dismissed as illusory.

—

In Kaschnitz's note: The son who brought the flames before the patients' eyes to the tree so as to burn it, is joined by a second son. It is he (Robert), who stops the fire-bearer that night, and who, according to Kaschnitz, will lie down in front of a train a short time later.

A print that the artist Ernst Ludwig Kirchner made in 1917 or 1918 during his stay in the closed ward for twenty-six male patients: *The Head of Robert Binswanger (the Student)*. A woodcut of the boy's face: side part, eyes wide.

—

The next day, as Kaschnitz is walking across the grounds of the asylum, she meets Vaslav Nijinsky, the Russian dancer, about whom it was said at the beginning of the last century that no one could leap like him, rising high into the air and seeming to pause there for a moment. Or crossing his legs five times over.

Nijinsky, performing for the last time on January 19, 1919, at the Hotel Suvretta in St. Moritz: He would now dance the war, he said, and actually looked as if he were dancing for his life. In the days that followed, he wrote in his diary.

"I will build a bridge between Europe and America that will not be expensive," he writes.

And: "I sat in an aeroplane and cried."

On March 4 of the same year, Nijinsky was brought to the mental asylum Burghölzli, later to be transferred to the sanatorium on the lake where, as Joseph Roth said, "the orderlies were as tender as midwives."

—

The Radetzky March: Every six months, the factory owner Taußig, who suffers from a "mild, supposedly cyclical disorder," checks into the asylum, where "spoiled madmen from wealthy families" receive the tender treatment of the orderlies.

—

In winter back then as I followed the shore path by the former sanatorium, steam hung over the surface of the water, and the roads were coated with a thin, nearly invisible layer of ice. In the evenings through the flurries, the taillights of the cars stopped at the railroad crossing, engines idling. I was listening to "Turiya and Ramakrishna" on my headphones; at night I watched TV.

—

In the third-floor basement of the Central Library is a Kaschnitz biography from 1992. The first part ("Forests of Childhood") is preceded by three lines:

And quickly the time was my time.
Whoever came to the world drawn by horses
Left it in a spaceship.

I sat in an aeroplane and cried.

Page 21: Kaschnitz, as a child when she was still Marie Luise von Holzing-Berstett, or rather called herself EIRAM ESIUL, rang for the nanny, Lulu, "who comes to the room with some consoling sugar water."

Page 24: Regarding her story "The Fat Child," she tells Horst Bienek that she herself had also been an "obedient, sleepy, and overfed child," "but also one with many fears, and one who started howling at every opportunity."

No indication of a visit to the gardens of the sanatorium.

—

Roughly seven or eight years before the psychiatrist's son—illuminated by the fireworks spreading into ever new and bright formations in the air—carries the flickering candles through the garden, the patient whom Binswanger will give the name "Ellen West" is admitted to the Bellevue sanatorium in Kreuzlingen on January 14, 1921.

And in the windows, Kaschnitz writes, the patients stood and clapped.

And the orderlies were as tender as midwives.

One fall, before her arrival on the southern shore of Lake Constance on October 21, 1920, West wrote in her diary, "From time to time new circumstantial evidence comes to me: for instance, when I arrive at an empty hotel room, I want to eat something first."

—

Germany journey. Mannheim, Cologne, Münster. Blue sky over Westphalia. The trees outside Recklinghausen are tall and close to the tracks, the underside of their leaves glowing silver in the warm October light.

The night before, I ran out of the house again at about one o'clock; suddenly, hundreds of bats were circling the floodlights of the empty Letzigrund stadium. Individual animals zooming out of the spotlight into the darkness and flying low over me. Craning my neck, the white fur of their bellies appears in perfect clarity. In front of the Lion Bar, a red Lamborghini Aventador with open scissor doors.

And I immediately took these animals, and the car, as a sign, again in reference to C.: As if they were bearers of a message I had been expecting for a long time (J'ai faim. / Je t'aime.). Although he, C., was lying on the bed at the time listening to the album *Persian Surgery Dervishes*, almost certainly suspecting nothing.

When I arrive at the empty hotel room, I'm hungry. Through the open window, the noise of vehicles 200 meters off speeding down the German highway, through the Münsterland and toward the Baltic or Leverkusen, the Vulkaneifel triangle and the Saarkohlenwald.

The great shadows of horses running through the park landscape.

At some point, late, the flashing display of the phone (*DataRoaming*).

Early in the morning, I wander through the dark corridors of the hotel with wet hair in search of the exit. The urgent desire to always speak of C., to have all sentences be secretly about C., even when, for example, the receptionist asks me if I've had anything from the minibar. On the bus to the train station, women with big baskets as if they're all going mushrooming.

—

When I saw C. for the first time: we were in the streetcar holding onto the poles above our heads.

Once, later, when I was on the escalator in Letzipark.

How even then, in each of those moments, a shocking light spread over everything, the light that changes what appears, the light toward which the blind pilgrim pitches herself in the pine grove with thousands of others, entirely outside of herself: an éclat.

—

This stupid transformation of the world in a pine grove. Which is nonetheless very beautiful.

—

Coffee with Erika, my neighbor from the second floor. She used to work in the café on the premises of the Maag gear factory, which closed in the '90s.

While we're talking, I'm already marching off again secretly, right into the aforementioned forest.

Erika with her beautiful little creole hoop earrings that still glint from far away through the spaces between the trees.

All the birds are already there.

—

And everything shines and radiates and is one big promise:

I lie on beds of moss and with wide eyes I contemplate everything: He (C.) abides in all things, and that is why I love all things so much.

And never have I seen a forest so insanely brightly lit, I say to my friends: For a year and a half I haven't once shut my eyes.

For days I lounge around in the shade of the trees or climb one plateau after another, and before I reach the peak, I watch, exhilarated, as a group of birds fly in V-formation across the center of the sun.

The peaks called *crisis* by Lady Chatterley.

It's true that I also cry a lot in this forest, I say to my friends, who express their skepticism. I'm often hungry and tired and alone — in particular, I have misplaced my pens in a moment of ecstasy.

—

Deborah Levy in her response to George Orwell's "Why I Write": "The night before, when I had walked into the forest at midnight, that was what I really wanted to do. I was lost because I had missed the turn to the hotel, but I think I wanted to get lost to see what happened next."

29

—

Suddenly I thought again of the forest in EIRAM ESIUL's story "The Fat Child," and of the titular child with her cool, bright eyes who suddenly enters the narrator's apartment one winter afternoon.

The child eats the bread that the woman has prepared for herself: Like a caterpillar, it says, the child eats everything the woman reluctantly serves, and the noises the child makes in the process arouse anger and also despair in the woman, who regards the child with suspicion—dark feelings, indeed.

Later while skating, the child breaks through the ice and stands in the icy water up to her waist, where her sister was executing perfect figure eights just a moment ago. As the narrator, standing on the icy jetty, doubts whether the fat child will succeed in pulling herself out of the water, she sees that something is happening to the child's face: Surrounded by the dark water, the child suddenly seems to drink up all the life in the world, seems to want to drink, and she begins with effort to heave her heavy body out of the water:

"a terrible struggle for liberation and transformation, like the breaking open of a shell or a web..."

and the lake that day is, as ever, surrounded by black woods, just as the narrator remembered it from the jetty in her childhood.

—

The husband of the patient EW informs the treating psychiatrist, LUDWIG BINSWANGER (Kreuzlingen), that even as a child his wife had found it "interesting to have a fatal accident, for example, to fall through the ice while skating."

Binswanger also notes in his case study that she was a stubborn, violent child. "Once she was shown a bird's nest; but she declared firmly that it was not a bird's nest, and would not be dissuaded." She wishes she were a boy, rides a horse negligently, kisses children with scarlet fever, sets herself up "naked on the balcony after a warm bath," climbs "with a fever of 102 degrees in an easterly wind onto the front of a streetcar."

"Nowhere does she care about the judgment of the world," Binswanger writes in her life and illness history. On the contrary, in her eighteenth year, she notes in a diary "how the Count, while speaking, slowly crushed his fine bread in his hand," this casualness of wealth and waste, while she imagines the figure of a hungry person, standing outside in the cold.

At twenty, she travels overseas: a stay on the North American continent she left with her parents and two brothers as a child, when the family emigrated to Europe. "She eats and drinks with pleasure," Binswanger records. "This is the last time she'll eat without harm. Then she gets engaged to a romantic from abroad, but allows the engagement to be called off at her father's request. On the return journey she stops in Sicily, continuing to work on a paper 'On the Professions of Women,' loves life (according to her diary) passionately, her pulse hammering all the way into her fingertips…"

—

Shortly before eight thirty, the ship reaches the harbor entrance of Messina. In front of us, standing tall in the morning sun, a golden Madonna reaches out her right hand in blessing. The Madonna della Lettera, *says the German, who spent much of last night on deck with his border collie and now returns to the railing with a cup of coffee from the ship's interior, Madonna of the Letter, who blessed the city in the year of 42 BCE in writing. The Italians! He lets his arm sweep over the landscape before us. Ah, the Catholics and their devotion to the Mother of God.*

From a distance I see my friends standing in the shadow of the terminal, K. with her arms folded, S. leaning against the outer wall of the building. I can see on them the time they've spent on the island. They talk casually while they wait, because they have already seen everything around them: sleeping animals, dead animals, incoming ships, rotting vegetable matter, water poured from plastic buckets over the uneven square flowing in black rivulets into the cracks and holes in the asphalt, then slowly evaporating over the course of the day.

We follow a narrow street paved with large stones. The owner of the guesthouse, says K., a woman around sixty named Beatrice, sits all day at a large table in front of her house, one grandchild or another on her lap; next to her, her daughter who is looking for work, or the son-in-law, a long-haired Frenchman from Toulouse, from whom the daughter has long since separated, but who maintains the sympathies of his mother-in-law, more or less. He wears shorts and clowns around with his daughter or strokes the female guests' necks with his index finger as he passes. It is impossible to enter or leave the inn without being ordered to this table by Beatrice to drink at least an espresso, which Beatrice's daughter reluctantly prepares each time. The grandchildren, with their dusty hands and feet and their long French hair, roll into one's lap—climbing you like they climb walls or hills—and run their hands over the faces of each of the inn's guests as if blind—blind children trying to determine who they know among present company. Among the guests, says S., are those who thoroughly enjoy Beatrice's austere form of hospitality: some German backpackers, a volcano researcher and his girlfriend who just photographed the crater of Stromboli and are now waiting for their flight back to Turin, have all settled in at the table. Every morning, they take their usual places and chat while simultaneously cutting figs into quarters, checking the weather forecast on their phones, or stroking the fur of the cats lying lazily around. To outsiders, K. says, their association with Beatrice's family seems private, even familial. Not least, the confidential, if not intrusive manner in which the Frenchman deals with the guests to the displeasure of Beatrice's daughter causes all boundaries to blur.

The Frenchman—says S.—calls both his mother-in-law and his ex-wife Mamma.

I eat and drink with pleasure. Beatrice has her daughter serve olives and crudo. The wine tastes pleasantly bitter. I allow my glass to be refilled by the Frenchman, who wears no shoes and always keeps an eye out for glasses that need filling. After a certain number of glasses, my pulse pounds all the way to my fingertips. For a short time, I say, I was engaged to a man from overseas, but that is now a thing of the past. Beatrice's daughter wipes a child's sticky mouth with a handkerchief. She smokes thin cigarettes and plays with the pack with her free hand. S. has a student of philosophy from Bielefeld explain the structure of Sicilian society to him. I'm working on a text about women's professions; at night I listen to "Turiya and Ramakrishna" on my headphones.

Around four o'clock in the morning—says Clara, the volcano researcher's girlfriend—Stromboli again ejected large quantities of lava. She had seen pictures showing that many of the island's inhabitants had gone out into the dark sea in small motorboats when it happened.

In front of the steep flank of the volcano, the Sciara del Fuoco, *they rocked on the black, almost jet-black, water, before them the insanely hot, orange-glowing mass flowing continuously over the crater rim down into the sea, where it produces tall, ghostly clouds of steam when it touches the water.*

When I step out of the house early in the morning and am about to pop a Concord grape in my mouth, Beatrice emerges noiselessly from the garden. She steps close, examines me, and then places her right hand on my stomach with an approving look. I remain motionless, the grape on my tongue.

Clara tells me she has the impression that the assembled company, Beatrice's court, is just waiting for the Frenchman to decide on one of the women present. When he went around touching the women's necks like that, it reminded her of a game they used to play: children sitting in a circle facing each other, behind them a child walking past with a piece of cloth or a crumpled handkerchief in her hand, which the child at some point drops as inconspicuously as possible behind another child's back. Interestingly—Clara says with a wrinkled brow—this Frenchman who has been running in circles behind our backs for days without dropping his handkerchief seems to have the whole group, herself included, in thrall, even though Clara is in no way interested in this man if for no other reason than that he never wears shoes, which in her view betrays a lack of style.

S. thinks that Beatrice is probably convinced I am pregnant and has given me her blessing with her hand, so to speak: mamma *to* mamma. *Madonna. K., on the other hand, believes that Beatrice simply doesn't care much for the widespread leanness of young women and that her intimate gesture was intended to express her joy at the fact that I enjoy life in all its opulence and show it.*

I loved life passionately, my pulse hammering to my fingertips; now I lie on the récamiere with eyes closed, thinking about the vocation of woman and the Frenchman's handkerchief. I ate and drank with pleasure: now the time of figs and grapes is over.

S. and the Frenchman have left for an evening walk on the pier. Beatrice's daughter lights a cigarette and throws her head back as she exhales the smoke, as if watching the signs, the signals she sends. On the bench against the wall of the house, her daughter lies sleeping, her knotted, stringy hair falling in her face. Clara's boyfriend covers her with his North Face jacket and heads to bed.

The crickets in the Italian woman's garden. The Madonna of the letter with the three fingers of her right hand spread. The women's clothes on the day of the shore leave. Sleeping animals, dead animals, rotting vegetable remains.

Clara said that on the island of Stromboli she encountered the same woman every morning in the village store: a tall, serious woman of perhaps twenty-seven years of age. She spoke broken Italian and always bought cigarettes and fruit, sometimes a loaf of bread. There was something hard and angular in this woman's features; she wore her hair in a buzz cut, and despite the heat, she always had on heavy shoes. Well, said Clara, I liked this woman, and for a few days I imagined how she must have lived and traveled; I saw her riding in the back seat of cabs through giant Asian cities or drinking red wine in the dining car of a European night train as it passed through Mannheim, Frankfurt, Fulda, engrossed in Sigfried Giedion's Mechanization Takes Command *or Paul Lafargue's* The Right to Be Lazy. *Although I of course knew this was all nonsense, I thought of that woman as a warrior—a person who, if*

threatened, could single-handedly ensure her own sur-
vival; indeed, I was positive that she lived alone, that
she spent her life alone; even her size made it seem like
she wouldn't fit into any conventional arrangement.

Beatrice's daughter laughs at this point, she brushes
a strand of hair off her forehead and then stands up to
top us and herself off.

Well, said Clara, in the end, two or three days
before we left, my boyfriend and I were sitting in the
courtyard of the little church, where the neighbors and
tourists gather every night to sit on the little wall and
steps leading up to the church and look out on the wa-
ter, when the warrior woman appeared, accompanied
by a man. They sat down close to each other on the
wall, and I saw in an instant that this was a beautiful,
gentle man with whom the woman seemed to live. This
sight shook me so much in some way that in the days
that followed, I compulsively recalled this moment in
front of the church. Above all, I felt a ridiculous but pro-
found jealousy of this woman, whose appearance I now
no longer admired, but experienced as a provocation:
she, who had not observed any of the rules and, rather
than playing the game with the handkerchief, had trav-
eled the world in dining cars instead; she, who had left
the handkerchief where it lay or pitched it in a trash
can at a train station, had escaped the intended pun-
ishment for her self-indulgence, her size, and her hard
features—to live from then on and for all time alone.
On the contrary, Clara said, she had found this gentle
man who not only had the capacity to accept all that
this woman was, but loved and desired her. For what? I
thought for days in my jealousy, while my boyfriend and

I observed the volcano and ate large capers, what did I do all this for? What I meant by that I didn't quite know myself—a form of abstinence perhaps, which I now understood had affected my life to a much greater degree than I had ever realized.

Beatrice's daughter carries her sleeping child inside the house and, when she returns, finishes her glass in great gulps. Here, she said, seemingly without addressing anyone, in the strait between the island and the mainland, two monsters have lurked since time immemorial: Scylla, who carries off the men from passing ships; and Charybdis, who drags everything into the depths to satisfy her monstrous hunger—ferries and their freight, live animals, automobiles, cocktail glasses, sailors. Before she was hurled into exile here, they say Charybdis lived on land, just like us, but she was hungry, always hungry, so hungry that she took Hercules's cattle and devoured them.

Around 2 AM K. enters my room and says that S. has not yet returned from her walk with the Frenchman. Beatrice's daughter had fallen asleep in front of the television. K. sits down on the edge of the bed and makes her hair into a braid. Are you hungry too? she asks. Yes, I say, but the time for figs and good ham is over now.

—

Late at night: Klaus Kinski drinking condensed milk in *Burden of Dreams* (1982). He cannot bring himself to drink the drink (masato) that the women in the Peruvian

38

rainforest prepare by first chewing the root tubers of the cassava plant and then spitting them out.

—

E. West, p. 67: "2. When I realize how much I can eat, a terrible fear of myself is awakened in me. A fear of the animal in me. A fear of something boundless into which I am in danger of sinking."

In Bourdieu: The Berbers in Kabylia said of someone who has slept with a woman that he "has eaten and drunk."

—

With Paul in the Aldi in Stötteritz: He runs back and forth between the shelves—port wine, clementines, bread, beer, milk, spinach, jams. I say that Ellen West put it like this: "We explained it this way in the analysis: I try to satisfy two things when I eat: hunger and love."

Through the silent streets we carry the groceries home. Just like when I still lived here: the scattered lights in windows of the tall houses, between them the dark parts, uninhabited floors, abandoned objects.

When you walked home at night, you sort of groped your way from lamp to lamp.

—

Sudden memory of the last New Year's Eve: I dreamed of a trip along the coast of the Ionian Sea, saw glimmering landscapes, hills bathed in summer light, promenades, towns, supermarkets, the white minarets of a mosque. Young people accompanied me on their scooters; together we spiraled up the SH8 ever higher into the mountains.

As if every dream was about C. or as if he, C., conversely could transform into anything: animals, cosmic matter, landscape.

And then a memory of how, on January 1, I went up the Rietberg with Laura; below us, the lake was quite festive, the last fireworks climbing the early afternoon air. We read that Ernst Ludwig Kirchner wrote in July 1919 of the young Zurich artist Alice Boner: "Tender female student. Wine, cigarettes. [...] Seeks love and puts it into the landscape."

The city was so quiet and empty on that first day of the year. I returned home with my hands in my coat pockets, and as I crossed the deserted Fritschi Park, I remembered that when he, C., had first entered my apartment, he was suddenly very hungry, as he freely admitted; he opened all my drawers and cupboards, even the freezer.

—

"Dream 3: Dreams that she jumped into the water through a ship's hatch while traveling overseas. Her first lover (the student) and her current husband made resuscitation attempts. She ate a lot of chocolates and packed her bags.

Dream 4: She orders goulash, says she is very hungry, but only wants a small portion. Complains to her old nanny that she is being tortured a lot. Wants to set herself on fire in the forest."

—

Ellen West, born "overseas" in 1888, moved to Europe as a child with her family, which was said to be Jewish and wealthy. "Her games were boyish until she was 16. She preferred going around in trousers."

After returning from a second trip to America at the age of twenty, with a detour via Sicily, and developing during her time on the island "a huge appetite," she begins to starve herself, setting out on increasingly extensive walks. If her friends stop along the way, Binswanger reports, she walks in circles around them, continuously circling so as to keep moving.

Letter to Emma: "There is in general a great shame in me that I am so ruled by an idea which must seem unspeakably ridiculous and contemptible to all sensible people."

It is said in the research that the decision to eat or not involves an obsession with death; the patient EW had negotiated the question of life or death using the example of eating; there is talk of *great depression*, of m e l a n c h o l i a , obsession de la honte du corps, anorexia nervosa, the alienation of woman under patriarchy, a reduction of the concept of the world to the shape of a hole, of a pronounced orality, the desire for assimilation, for fulfillment. In the case study published by Binswanger in the war years 1944/45 we find the "equations" (A) slim = intellectual; fat = Jewish and bourgeois; and (B) eating = fertilized and pregnant.

"In the case of Ellen West, too," writes Binswanger, "the craving for fulfillment showed itself by no means only in the form of food cravings and hunger, but in the form of her craving for life and power, her hunger for life and power ('ambition') in general." West bites "lustily into all life."

"Oh, that I were a boy, a boy" (EW, March 1902).

—

On the phone with A., I talk about the fat kid I saw yesterday in a fast food restaurant: With a hat pulled down low on his face, he sits in front of a mountain of fried potatoes and talks incessantly to his mother, voicing the desire in almost imploring tones to return here after death and eat potatoes forever.

Because that's how the child imagines heaven: fried potatoes in excess.

—

At lunch, C. thinks that the most passable way to write about EW again, after so many have already done so, is perhaps to turn away completely from analysis and studies: the woman whose name we don't know—Jewish, bilingual, well-to-do—who gets engaged twice and breaks off both engagements at her father's request; for whom no horse is too dangerous; who reads and is interested in politics; who first wants to foment revolution and feels called to improve the world ("Make concessions, you preach? I don't want to make any concessions! You see that the existing social order is rotten, rotten to the root, dirty and mean, but you do nothing to change it."); who "like a Russian nihilist, [wants to] leave home and family, live among the poorest of the poor, and create propaganda for the great cause"; who then plunges headlong into the depths again, good for nothing and dark, filled with longing, denying herself food in the early twentieth century despite her desire, her great appetite, and becomes an ascetic, forever in temptation.

"Let me briefly describe a morning. I am sitting at my desk and working. I have much to do, much that I've been looking forward to. But an agonizing restlessness denies me peace. I jump up, run back and forth, stopping over and over in front of the cupboard where my bread is. I eat some; ten minutes later I jump up again and eat some more. I firmly resolve not to eat any more. [...] Most of the time I end up running out into the street. I run away from the bread in my cupboard [...] and stumble aimlessly about."

As we sit by the window drinking coffee after dinner, we read Thomas Bernhard's description of his acceptance of the Grillparzer Prize in Vienna: How, on the day of the ceremony, Bernhard tries on a new suit in the changing room of *Sir Anthony*, which—a few brief hours later, after a meal with friends and his aunt at the Gösser Bierklinik—he finds to be quite obviously too tight, "at least a whole size too small" and returns to the store the same day to exchange it for a larger size.

"After a meal," I say as I close the book, EW writes that she "always feels worst of all." Feelings of emptiness, fear, and helplessness.

Elsewhere, "As soon as I feel a pressure at the waist—I mean pressure from the waistband of my skirt—my mood sinks and I get such a severe depression, as if I were dealing with who knows what all kind of tragic things."

While C. is lacing up his shoes, I tell him that EW thought she would find liberation if she could only solve the riddle presented by "the association of food with longing."

Schneverdingen

– So I spent that winter near the former sanatorium on the lake. One of my aunts came to visit after a few weeks. She had heard from my mother about my stay and then, on a whim, drove here in her Renault Twingo, she said. She stood downstairs in the cold and rang the doorbell, her head craned back. I have always liked this eldest sister of my mother; at every opportunity she burst into boisterous laughter—in principle she seemed to be examining the doings, indeed the being, of others at any opportunity. Every time I saw her, for example, she would ask me a series of factual questions, the laughter already in her eyes and in her throat, ready for me to finally give it cause to burst forth with one of my answers.

As she stood in front of the house and rang the bell, I was sitting on the second floor bent over my notes, my research; then, all of a sudden, my living, breathing aunt stepped into its midst, and when I later found myself eating with her at Drachenburg Restaurant, it seemed only logical.

– The inclusion of the biographical?

– Yes. So to raise the question of my own origins, my own point of departure.

I think we were eating schnitzel, Rosi and I, and as I watched her cut the meat into pieces we talked about simple, bright things, and I thought the research would rightly start with my mother and her siblings' hands.

Like, for example, on my mother's sixty-third birthday: one of my aunts tells me when I ask, that as children they had to hold the pigs when they were stunned; the other aunt contests the truth of the story, saying that they only vacuumed sausages, delivering the meat and so on; in other words, helped with the processing. My uncle arrives late, he had to dress a freshly shot deer— he says as he gets out of his dusty Volvo.

The older I get, the more my own hands begin to resemble those of my mother. Not fine, not elegant, but not coarse either. Practical hands that can handle a knife and separate meat from bone.

– And kill?

– Yes, that too.

The killing of animals. And we do eat them daily, I don't have any illusions. I maintain that it's not fundamentally reprehensible. But it's a fact that for generations my family on my mother's side practiced slaughtering and butchering in the meat processing business. And that's where these hands of mine come from, which I've only recently realized.

And what interests me is what else these hands could do, what else they know.

– Desire?

– Yes, of course.

—

I know a foreign, a far-flung territory, I write to C., where dwarf quail lay small, shiny eggs and wild herds of palomino roam shady woods, red-eyed tortoises heave their bodies over smoothly polished warm stones, silvery doves zip around my head in a flurry as I sit on a woven chair in the heat eating supper, etc. If it pleased you to visit me there, I write, after dinner we could lie down in the shade of the monstera.

—

The figure of a woman in Joyce: "She sat at the window watching the evening invade the avenue. Her head was leaned against the window curtains and in her nostrils was the odour of dusty cretonne." A ship is anchored in the city's harbor at this time, the so-called night ship, which will depart in a few hours and carry its European passengers across the Atlantic to Buenos Aires.

The woman, Eveline, remembers at that moment her mother's last night: how she lies dying in the narrow, dark sickroom and repeats the same words without end—"Derevaun Seraun! Derevaun Seraun!"—she keeps calling out to her, the daughter, as Joyce writes, with foolish persistence.

The meaning of the words, Wim Tigges writes in the fall of 1994 under the title *"Derevaun Seraun!" Resignation or Escape?* in the *James Joyce Quarterly*, is unclear: Don Gifford notes that Patrick Henchy finds in it the Gaelic formulation, "The end of pleasure is pain." Roland Smith, on the other hand, renders the sentence in English as "The end of the song is raving madness"; Marian Lovett of the University of Limerick allegedly translated the exclamation spontaneously as

"I have been there; you should go there" (do raibh ann, siar ann).

The memory of the dark, sibylline speech of the dying mother as a reminder to follow the sailor onto the night ship and to the so-called "New World" after all; the mother's words as an expression of her veiled, secret, or never realized desire.

—

As I walk around my apartment watering the plants, I say to A. on the phone: After midnight, I wake up and I'm hungry. I leave my cabin and walk the decks of the night ship, following the stairs and corridors down into the depths of the craft, and as I pass the crew's mess, I see a choir standing there, in front of festively set tables; from their midst, my mother emerges. Dreamily, she smiles, cheeks flushed, and sways gently back and forth. "The end," sings my mother in her beautiful, clear soprano, "the end of pleasure is pain." The chief officer from Schneverdingen, sitting on the corner bench, hides his face in his hands in distress. Then the choir starts up.

—

"I am afraid of boundlessness. They say that you are most afraid of the things you most desire. [...]
Is that why I dream so often of water?"
EW, 27 Oct. 1920.

"And it seemed she was like the sea, nothing but dark waves rising and heaving, heaving with a great swell, so that slowly her whole darkness was in motion…"

D. H. Lawrence, *Lady Chatterley's Lover*, p. 172.

—

The mother, I say to A., just speaks in tongues, I think. She speaks in code to communicate to the daughter: I knew a foreign, a very beautiful place; partridges wander there through the shady grove, red-eyed turtles lie motionless in the stagnant water, silvery doves nest in the crowns of tall trees, and so on, go and see.

—

The territory to which Madame Bovary is transported at night by four horses: New lands, whole cities "with domes, bridges, ships, lemon groves, and cathedrals of white marble" lie before her; she dreams of fruit stacked into pyramids, of pale statues, and of the shadows of palm trees by the sea.

—

Or the other way around: the mother warns the daughter, Eveline, not to leave her country, "that valley of the shadow," as Ursula K. Le Guin called it, the tangled, animalistic, impure night-side of the country, so familiar to women (location of the irrational and irreparable, of illness and weakness).

For if there was a day side to this shadow valley, "high sierras, prairies of bright grass," it was known to the women at most from stories (*pioneers' tales*)

and not to be achieved by imitating *Machoman*. (Le Guin 1983)

Viewed in this way, I say, Eveline's final refusal to follow the sailor onto the night ship also adds further meaning to her mother's exclamation on her deathbed: the woman does not take part in the voyage of discovery, the expedition, although she would also like to see the partridges, the sleeping turtles, but stays at home because she already suspects: the end of the song is *raving madness*, death and destruction overseas.

—

How does Freud put it again; doesn't he describe the sexual life of women as a "dark continent"?

—

Telephone call with A. The cretonne curtain covering Eveline's window already contains, if you like, the overseas territory: the European undertaking in the New World, plantations of the Greater Antilles and the American South, which supplied cotton to the factories of Europe across the Atlantic.

—

I wake up after midnight and descend the stairs of my parents' home. From the hallway I see that there is still a light on in the kitchen, which doesn't surprise me, because my mother, an elementary school teacher, spent many of my childhood nights working at the kitchen table; when I was a teenager, if I got up late in the evening to pour myself a glass of milk in the kitchen, or when returning home late after drinking Baileys from water glasses with my girlfriends to fall asleep in front of the television, I'd find her there, with scissors and pencils, bent over the notebooks of her students. Now, as I approach the kitchen, I see that my mother is standing upright behind the table, a white apron tied around her, a knife in her right hand. As I enter the room, she wipes her forehead with the back of her hand, leaving a bloody streak on her exhausted face. Then she puts the knife back to work and, with the utmost concentration, cuts the piece of meat on the table in front of her into small cubes. I take a seat. Outside there is snow. The branches of the four apple trees in the garden bend under its weight. Silently and beautifully, the midnight winter landscape spreads out beyond my mother. "I have been there; you should go there," she says, following my gaze, the bloody knife in her hand.

Or did she say "do raibh ann, siar ann"; I don't know anymore.

—

How, about three years ago I was walking from the shore of a lake to the S-Bahn station early in the morning. Icy

51

cold wind under my coat, up my sleeves, into my face. An older man is standing in front of the bakery at the station He instantly comes running up to me, asks for money, and then says, while he jumps from one leg to the other, freezing, that if it was true I was a writer, we'd have to meet again next Monday at half past two so that I could write down his story and that of his father, who had been a butcher.

Wholesaler or employee, he asks when I say that my grandfather was also a butcher.

—

After midnight I walk home through the empty streets, past the towers of the Hardau II housing complex and the deserted stadium, across the meadows in the park. On a bench someone sits with his kit and cooks up. At home, I fall asleep on the sofa, a pillow tucked under my neck, with the light on: In a dream, C. opens all my drawers and cupboards, even the freezer, but doesn't find whatever he's in the mood for; nothing that appeals to him, so we run to the supermarket and buy blood oranges, wine, stuffed peppers, asparagus canapés, salmon and oysters, frozen escargot, pickled artichoke hearts, a good dozen passion fruits.

About the refrigerator, A. says he recently read, "A look in the fridge is considered an intimate act."

In Achternbusch: "Since then, I don't let anyone get to me, so that absolutely none of my energy is diverted."

The birds whistle *chee fee chee fee chee fee*.

—

"Ellen skips entire meals, then indiscriminately pounces with all the greater desire on any food that happens to be at hand. She consumes several pounds of tomatoes and twenty oranges daily." (Binswanger, p. 265)

—

In the tale of the half pear, a pear and cheese are served at the end of a sumptuous meal at the king's court: to be precise, one pear for every two guests, and the knight— who had shone in the tournament the king had orga- nized at his daughter's request and was therefore seated next to the princess—takes the pear, cuts it in half and gobbles down his half without peeling it or first handing the other half to the king's daughter.

O chevalier, the princess later taunts the pear eater, *who threwe the pear unpeeled in his mouthe*.

How the king's daughter loudly proclaims the knight's embarrassing desire all over the tournament square.

In the same story (l. 495) the desire of the woman is *the great wickedness*.

—

– What are the things you learned from your mother?

– A certain rigor. Attention. A willingness to sacrifice. But also how to care for oneself.

– And in a practical sense?

– Well, what you learn. The performance of everyday activities, the use of things like scissors and paintbrushes. Also writing maybe; I'm not sure. In most cases, I'm quite unsure who taught me what, for example, skiing. On the whole, I don't remember it at all. Only riding a bike: I see myself riding a white BMX on summer evenings down the street and across the cul de sac toward the meadow without training wheels for the first time. How my parents first ran along and held the saddle, then let go. The very soft light of the early evenings, how the meadows in the distance merged seamlessly into the sky and how long that time of twilight seemed.

– Were you told about sex by your mother?

– Yes, my mother always spoke pretty freely. In that sense, there wasn't a single moment of enlightenment, but whenever we asked something (i.e., how does this and that actually work), we got an answer. Basically, I don't remember a time when I didn't know, when I was left wondering.

– Did that give you a sense of self-confidence, since you probably knew more than others as a child?

– No, I just took note, if I remember correctly. These things then lost any hint of spectacle, so it became more about technical knowledge. Desire, lust…that was something completely different.

– When did that start for you?

– I can't say exactly. When I was nearly five, my father took my sister and me to Italy, near Follonica. We spent a week or two there vacationing in a tourist village for people with kids, there were children's activities with music and sports and things like that, and I remember that there were two men. They must have been young, maybe in their early twenties or even younger, who worked as hosts and entertainers. And what I remember is that once, when we were drawing, we children broke out in a kind of frenzy and began to draw on those two young Italians, their feet and legs and so on, until the parents at some point intervened, and that it was mainly about the bodies of those men. That's such an early memory. I can still see their calves, which were very hairy and tanned from the Tuscan sun, their feet too, but not their faces.

—

I click through the internet and a thirty-five-year-old man from Hesse writes to me that he imagines his boss at the bank, who is black, a large black man, penetrating with his cock first me and then him, kneeling on the floor behind his desk. Could you love a man like me, baby, he writes, I mean in real life, could you, baby? I put on some coffee. Are you Southern, baby? he writes. In Brinkmann somewhere, I remember he calls it *dust south, concrete south, southern construction, to flee to the south, where the south is, from reality into the*

fiction called "South" and so forth.

—

By the way, I say to A. on the phone, that evening when C. visited me for the first time and inspected my refrigerator, he then made a meal in my kitchen. We ate and drank (the low table lamp illuminated only the lower part of his face—his mouth—while his eyes remained in the dark), and at about two o'clock in the morning he left to go home. That same night I woke suddenly at 4:30 with the image of the Vienna Secession before my eyes, the golden dome of the building and its white façade, as I had seen them in the glaring June light a few years before, when I had seen an exhibition of James Lee Byars's drawings in the small chamber on the upper floor and spent a long time walking around among the inscribed pennants, the golden flags, his letters sent to Switzerland.

—

How we once spent an entire night drinking in the hot kitchen and then finally opened the doors to the balcony around two in the morning: In the branches of the plane tree in the courtyard hung a blue towel, or maybe a blue soccer jersey; nothing was moving, everything seemed at a standstill, there was hardly any cool air entering the room, and someone said (he or I) that on the news it was reported that the water level of the lakes was low; soon the trees would drop their fruit because of the heat, and in the warm streams the graylings would die. How beautiful it was, that night, that summer in general. Above us the deep blue vault, and at the same time the fish had to be taken out of the water so that they wouldn't perish.

—

Day after day, I say to A. on the phone, I wake up in the same position, my legs folded close to my body, arms to my chest, as if protecting myself in my sleep. I look around my bedroom, amazed that I have spent the night just passed alone, that I was, just moments before, asleep in my bed, and the room expands before my eyes into a cathedral in which high above a bird flutters, *flap flap*.

Looking back on those nights, I'm startled by the image of myself in the evening, sitting alone at the kitchen table, washing the dishes, lying on the sofa, and falling asleep at some point, although I myself hardly ever give it a thought on those evenings; on the contrary, I was usually almost happy. It is, I think, perhaps no more than the astonishment that I had long since broken away of my own free will from my parents and was now an adult.

—

Mr. Williams (to the witness).—What is your daughter's name?—Ellen.

Do you have other children?—No.

What is her age, Mr. Turner?—She was fifteen on February 12, 1826.

Is her mother alive, Mr. Turner?—Yes, she is.

Is she in Lancaster?—Her mother?

Yes.—No, she is not.

What is the reason?—She is unwell.

Is it possible for her to make the trip?—That's not it.

—

In my dream, I'm traveling along the same coastline again; I pass the Strait of Otranto, and much later I see the outline of one of the Ionian Islands far out in the glittering sea. At the far end of this stretch of coast, two brothers sit in front of a two-story oval building built close to the water, its facade painted a bright blue—one runs the hotel he and his father built by hand, the other plays soccer in Dortmund and is just visiting. When I ask if I can get a room, the soccer player nods and strokes my hair tenderly. I lay my face against his warm throat.

Swan River

– I wanted to ask you again about *Capital*.

– Yes, it's such an interesting story that, as you know, I'm now consulting the book again. I bought the first volume in the Volksbuchhandlung Buch + Antik on Leipzig's Karl-Heine-Straße. It was the financial crisis, so around 2007, 2008, and I was living with Roman on Lütznerstraße at the time. I wrote during the day, and in the evenings, because of the extreme cold, we went to the pub.

– Did you all heat with coal?

– Yes, the coal was delivered in the fall and dumped into the basement through a small ground-level window from the street.

– Did you find that easy, the heating?

– The procedure was familiar to me from childhood. We heated with wood. And from fires in the forest. We had often done that as children, we lit all kinds of things on fire—mattresses, tires, plastic plates, plywood. But with the coal I was always afraid. It wasn't a very reasonable fear because our windows were super leaky and so fresh air always came through the cracks, but I was very afraid of closing the oven door too early and poisoning myself, like Sophie Taeuber-Arp who died like that in Max Bill's cabin.

– Did you read *Capital* during that time in Leipzig?

– Some chapters, the first chapters on use value and exchange value and so on—I certainly read those back then; 20 cubits of canvas = 1 skirt. And really it wouldn't be an exaggeration to say that all roads led me back there and also the story of the lottery player who won 1.7 million in the '70s and then lost it all. It's not easy to summarize it like that, but at some point I realized what really interested me had to do with a later episode in that man's life—when he traveled for some particular reason across the Atlantic to the Caribbean. Something seemed to reveal itself on that trip, for me at least, and I'm still working on that. But in any case, in this context, I went back and read in Marx the chapter on the modern theory of colonization. There he discusses a theory that a Brit named Wakefield developed in response to the question of how to produce wage laborers in the colonies. The problem, in a nutshell, was that there was so much free land in the overseas territories—free land in quotation marks, *desert*, Wakefield writes—and in principle anyone who came overseas from Europe could set up on their own and cultivate some land and so forth. Everyone could accumulate for themselves as independent producers instead of performing wage labor for a third party. So, in his theory of colonization, Wakefield attempts to answer the question of how these dependencies can be established anyway in order to secure the capitalists their labor force. And interestingly, Marx doesn't discuss slavery or the question of what it means that the plantation economy existed at the same time as the capitalist economic system.

– He writes in an earlier passage that "the veiled slavery of wage laborers in Europe needed the unqualified

60

slavery of the New World as its pedestal."

– And the social anthropologist Sidney Mintz writes of an irritation that befalls him when he sees the sugar cane fields and the white sugar in his cup simultaneously. Not primarily in the technical sense, because of the transformation, but because in the simultaneous sight of the sugar cane and the refined sugar a riddle or secret reveals itself—*the mystery*, he writes, that sugar production connects unknowns across time and space. Because, after all, sugar was historically produced on plantations but then consumed in Europe, including by European wage laborers.

So sugar is a motif or thing, a riddle that has come up time and again for me in recent years. For a long time I had a piece of paper above my desk with what I call "Dream 3" by Ellen West: she dreamed that she jumped through a ship's hatch into the water while traveling overseas. A student she once loved and her husband both try to revive her. Finally, "she ate a lot of chocolates and packed her bags."

—

Last night, on a balcony above the Limmatquai: someone explains that capitalism is dependent on divisions that are always newly executed and consolidated, even deepened—the division of the overseas slave and the European proletarian, of citizen and undocumented person, of the merely sick and the invalid, the division of the exploited in the metropolis from the colonial subjects, of the man as a factory worker from the woman as a machine of reproduction, and so on (as Federici has it for instance),

because this is the only way that the system can maintain itself in the face of the glaring discrepancy between the promises of capitalism and its actual, miserable conditions.

Downstairs on the street a police car drives at walking pace alongside the lazy river toward Central. Someone shows up with a bottle of wine, and C., who arrived late and then leaned in the doorway seeming unconcerned, now thinks there was also discussion in the literature about primary accumulation as the accumulation of differences and divisions, as far as he knows.

At that moment, I step forward, or maybe I just mean to. I pull a pear out of my coat pocket and offer it to him.
    The fruit gleams in the light of the streetlamps.
That's all I have, I whisper, it's a good pear, take it already. C. throws me a brief glance, then he guides my hand and with the pear to his mouth and bites wordlessly.

O chevalier, so great is my delicious wickedness

—

Once, in late August, after an evening meal, I climbed a hill above Zurich with some people, the lime trees up there dark, behind our backs the floodlights of the airport. We sat down on the little wall, our shoulders sometimes touching in the darkness, and now, in memory, I see the tiny cars accelerating over the Hardbrücke. How quickly as time passes.

Another time, we're watching the beginning of the new year from the Käferberg; heads craned back, we watch the rockets, while around us, children holding their parents' hands stumble over the uneven meadow.

Then a night in a bar in Germany with an American programmer who talks about Arnold Schönberg, *Shawnberg*, he says. Later, the walk through dark, deserted streets. The bright apartment blocks on Manteuffelstraße like icy cuboids, craggy peaks rising into the frosty darkness. The warmth inside an American sweatshirt. When I wake up in the late morning, the rooms as bright as day can be.

In January after my thirtieth birthday, I lie for days in the sparsely furnished Berlin room that I have sublet for a few weeks, reading magazines. The temperature has dropped well below zero, and day and night I wear the same wool sweater I bought five or six years earlier for a few euros on Knochenhauerstraße in Bremen. When I walk over the Spree to Ostbahnhof to buy bread and juice and slices of pizza at *Ditsch*, I hear the sound of ice floes bumping against each other and then drifting apart again. At night I dream.

I camp out unnoticed in the city; hardly anyone knows I'm here. The probability that I will meet an acquaintance or a friend by chance on the short route to the Ostbahnhof is small.

Just once I venture to the Volksbühne, where a play about love is being staged. An actor runs alone in a circle on an almost empty stage. No one in the subway; always the same cold wind in Köpenicker Straße, I push the snow in front of me with my shoes, eat a *BiFi* sausage from the vending machine on Heinrich-Heine-Straße.

On one of those clear, ice-cold nights, A. stands in front of the pharmacy on Hermannplatz and waits. As we walk together on Karl-Marx-Straße, I try to quote Poe from memory: *For some months I had been ill in health, but was now convalescent.* He had also—says A.—been ill until recently and had read American essays over Christmas. He had also dreamed: We wore wreaths, we walked long halls. Behind us, five international painting students sat on a sofa smoking joints. There were bouquets of flowers on the counters. Late at night I return to my room, take off all my clothes, and immediately fall asleep.

—

I know a place—I write to C.—I am standing there, at the edge of a clearing where a bunch of golden horses graze, and when they gallop past me, startled by the sound of a quail in the bushes, I jump out from between the trees, grab one of the large animals by its flaxen mane, and swing myself onto its back. Yellow-feathered saffron finches accompany us on our way through the woods, and I'm already looking forward to supper.

—

– I am constantly having these conversations with him, with C., in my head, starting one conversation after another with him, always new conversations even when I'm still half asleep. Then this morning, when I woke up and the sky was already very bright—a very fine brightness with a bit of haze, and on top of it, the smoke from the chimneys of the houses opposite—I started reading a second book by Peter Kurzeck. It begins with him at the end of January 1984 moving out of the home of the woman he lived with and her daughter—he has to go. He moves into a room in Frankfurt and in the middle of this room is a piano, a locked piano, and so he tries to sleep there. *A storage room*, he writes, *where I tried like a stranger to sleep. With caution. Temporarily. In the third person, so to speak*, and then I thought: I also just need to write everything down, for C., everything, the weather and the morning light from the direction of the lake and how the line of the hill at some point becomes visible through the haze. I thought: that would be enough then, the description of this morning, at least it would be enough for me; I'd be convinced…as I imagine someone delivering such a description to my mailbox. And it was such a beautiful day outside, so bright, like everything was starting all over again. That would be enough for me. As far as I'm concerned, I'd then be ready for anything.

—

When the Air France plane leaves the airport and climbs finally into the weatherless area of the atmosphere, the brightness penetrates the cabin so abruptly that my neighbor, who was just looking out the window, covers his eyes with a silent cry. Although we should know perfectly well, he says, his hands still protectively over his eyes, we forget the sun shines constantly at 10,000

meters. Just a few moments ago, he was watching the
airport workers standing around in the rain on the tar-
mac of Milano-Malpensa using their glow sticks, the
luminous instruments they use to show the planes the
way. He had drunk a coffee at a café bar in the coolly
lit terminal and watched the travelers who, step by step,
approached their destinations with their suitcases and
travel equipment. On this morning he found them all
pronouncedly ugly—their haircuts, indeed their whole
manner of existence, as well as their way of moving
through these halls, the presumption with which they
traveled, and the ugliest of all, he says, of course, nat-
urally, seemed to be himself when, just before boarding
the plane, he bent over a sink and looked in the mirror.
And now this light, he says, laughing almost noiselessly,
this stable blue. Then, as he turns to me, I see that he
has cool, light eyes.

The plane is already on approach to the Aéroport
Nantes Atlantique when he quietly remarks that he had
hoped for a cloudless day; he would have liked to have
seen this region from the air—the course of the Loire,
the western departments, perhaps some islands. And: In
the summer of 1849, an editor of the Neue Rheinische
Zeitung, *Freiligrath, sent a letter to Karl Marx when*
the latter was already in France and production of
the newspaper had ceased; if he was not mistaken, my
neighbor says, Freiligrath informed Marx in his letter
that a certain Dr. Daniels considered the department of
Morbihan—to which the French government wanted to
banish Marx—to be "the most unhealthy strip of France,
muddy and fever-breathing: the Pontine marshes of

Brittany." If he, Marx, obeyed the order, Freiligrath wrote, he would almost certainly come down with malaria, so it would be better if he went to England.

How beautifully this man with the cool, light eyes talks about the marshes, I think, while the flight attendants go down the rows and prepare the cabin for landing, and in an instant I am ready for anything: If he were to ask me now, I would say yes to everything, I would sign onto anything or sign over everything to him, I would follow him anywhere, even to the department of Morbihan.

—

In the bibliography of the first volume of *Capital*, two works by E. G. Wakefield: the two-volume *England and America*, published in 1833, from which Marx mockingly quotes in the twenty-fifth chapter on the theory of colonization, and the 1849 publication *A View of the Art of Colonization*. Also, there's a note that an edition of Adam Smith's *Inquiry into the Nature and Causes of the Wealth of Nations* was published with a commentary by Wakefield.

Previously, in 1831, his paper *Facts Relating to the Punishment of Death in the Metropolis*. The majority of the facts and all the scenes of horror depicted on the following pages, writes Wakefield in the preface, he gained from his own observation from May 1827 to May 1830 during his imprisonment in Newgate, the great London prison, and *terra incognita*.

("Ah, this is exactly how the imagination envisions

prison in times of barbarism," Flora Tristan noted in 1840 after her visit to Newgate in the *Promenades dans Londres,* which she later renamed *La ville monstre*. She reported a lack of daylight—only slowly did the eyes get used to the darkness in the cells.)

I had the opportunity, Wakefield explains in the second chapter, *NURSERIES OF CRIME,* to survey more than 100 thieves ranging in age from eight to fourteen about the direct causes that made them become thieves.

It does not begin spontaneously, the career of a thief, he writes. At the beginning there is seduction—in the form of food, for example, or other pleasures—and an experienced thief sometimes shells out up to ten pounds in a few days in order to corrupt a boy by taking him to the playhouse, allowing him to eat and drink extravagantly from the bakery, grocery, and pub. An even more effective form of seduction was the early arousal and gratification of sexual desire by women who collaborated with the thieves and whispered to the intoxicated boys that stealing was the only way to continue this life of unbridled debauchery.

Or, he writes, the child socializes with people, like the old women who run the fruit stands and cake shops. The child befriends the saleswoman and buys fruit and pieces of cake, until one day he comes without money: He will be cordially invited to help himself anyway and eat of the fine things, and he gets into debt in this way, deeper and deeper, until things are so far gone that he can easily be convinced by the shopkeeper or fruit seller to steal.

Soon, writes Wakefield, the young thief will prefer idleness and luxury to work and simple meals. He leaves his seductress or the fruit seller, "his original seducer, with whom he is no longer willing to share his plunder."

(Even well-behaved boys, the sons of decent business-people with good prospects for a hard-working and honest life…)

—

Ellen West in front of a bowl filled with twenty oranges.

The nanny comes into a room with sugarwater to comfort EIRAM ESIUL.

Me on the balcony above the Limmat, with the pear in hand, *still willing to share the fruit.*

—

Early morning, still dark, then the first light off the lake. "That was the first very cold night of the year," they say on the radio. Sitting yesterday evening with Natalie at the big window at Piazza: she wore beautiful woven earrings made of small beads, fried cutlets were brought from the kitchen. Now and then someone came inside, hood pulled deep over the face, eyes reddened by the cold. At some point I walked home— Zurlindenstraße, Brahmsstraße, nary a soul—then fell asleep immediately.

—

Wakefield:

John Williams, a twenty-three-year-old man, sentenced to death in Newgate for theft. Williams climbs up the pipe of a cistern on the morning of December 19, 1827, the day of his execution—perhaps, as some speculate, to drown himself in the cistern, but much more likely because he still hopes to escape his sentence this way. Williams falls into the cobbled courtyard and seriously injures his legs. Although everyone knows he is to be hanged that very day, a doctor tends to him carefully. As he is carried to the gallows, the blood begins to flow from his wounds again: it is clear to see.

Around noon, a phone call with A. Seagulls circle above the flat roof of the neighboring house. The heat makes the air shimmer. I say how the report on the conditions in Newgate and the implications of the death penalty ends with the chapter *TRANSPORTATION TO THE COLONIES*. In the majority of cases, death sentences were not carried out; the convicts were instead shipped to the colonies, to New South Wales, to Van Diemen's Land.

The prisoners of Newgate awaiting such a transfer were housed separately from the other inmates, Wakefield wrote, and they were more carefree, more cheerful: reports from the colonies—where the value of human labor exceeded any price and thus every convict transferred from the motherland was practically courted—those reports, which circulated among the prisoners, resounded with promise.

And time and again, he said, he had seen with his own eyes in Newgate how someone, after learning that he was to be taken to the colonies, suddenly recovered, developed an appetite, exhibited cheerfulness.

—

Around four in the morning I wake up, and outside is an orange light, everything strangely illuminated, and I think of how the blast furnaces of the Tevershall pit turn the sky red at night in *Lady Chatterley* and of the glow above the crater of Stromboli in summer a few years ago, but then I see that snow has fallen and reflects the light, casting it upward to create these new conditions.

I would like—I write that very night to C.—to invite you to dinner. I can be a generous hostess; I'll serve three courses, and at the end I'll offer cheese and fresh figs. Or we can direct ourselves, chatting and smoking, to the papaya tree, where I will separate the ripest fruit directly from the stem of the plant and open it with a longitudinal cut, revealing the black seeds surrounded by bright, sweet flesh which will be removed with a spoon.

—

As American lawyers say in court, "Strike that!" in order to withdraw a previously uttered question or a statement that pushes the boundaries of what is permissible to say.

How far out on a limb I have let myself go with these declarations, my invitations to C., for whom a pear seems to be nothing more than a thing hanging on a branch or lying in a green box in the supermarket.

Knock, knock,
I spy with my little eye
something whose juice when eaten runs down my chin and breasts,
oh my god I want another right now.

Strike that.

—

Australian Dictionary of Biography, volume 2, 1967: His survey of prisoners during his time in Newgate is what led Edward Gibbon Wakefield (1796–1862) to devote himself in the first place to emigration to the Antipodes and the urgent question of how to create wage laborers in the colonies.

In the colonies, writes Marx, Wakefield discovered that in order to be and remain one, the capitalist needs the worker as a complement; that is, Mr. Peel, who brings to the banks of the Swan River in New Holland investment capital of 50,000 pounds and 300 persons of the working class—men, women, and children, who shortly after their arrival disperse into the wide, promising country—is urgently dependent on the wage-laborer who is free and draws his water from the river.

When Mr. Peel—writes Wakefield—reaches Cockburn Sound with the provisions brought from England, he is, with some difficulty, just able to find laborers to place these goods under a shelter, but finding no one willing to undertake their onward transportation, the things remain there until they are spoiled; the tent rots.

"Unhappy Mr. Peel, who provided for everything but the export of English manufacturing conditions to the Swan River!"

Because a cotton gin is a machine for spinning cotton, Marx writes, it becomes capital only in certain relations. Voilà: capital is not a thing, but a social relation between persons mediated by things.

—

Through the courtyard of the prison walks a boy between eight and fourteen years old, two burning candles in his hands. In the windows stand the thieves, awaiting their transfer. John Williams lays his hands around the cistern pipe. On the shores of the Indian Ocean, Mr. Peel's tent slowly rots.

And Wakefield. On the morning of March 6, 1826, he arrives at the Albion Inn in Manchester, gives himself the alias Captain Wilson, has breakfast with his brother and his servant—a Frenchman—buys a second-hand green carriage, and sets off with his companions at two in the morning for Liverpool. Once there, they will lure fifteen-year-old Ellen Turner, heiress and only child of

William Turner of Shrigley Park, into the wrong carriage under false pretenses, transport her to Scotland, and at Gretna Green Wakefield will marry her for her fortune.

Trial of the Wakefields, examination of the father (William Turner):

I am now going to ask you some questions for form's sake, you will excuse my putting them to you. Are you in possession of landed property in the County of Chester? – I am.

I don't at all wish to know the particulars; you wont so understand me. Is that property considerable? – It is.

Now, besides furniture—I'm not speaking of particulars—but besides the furniture belonging to your house, are you in possession of personal property? – I am.

Well, again, I don't go into particulars at all, just so you understand me; is that considerable? – It is.

—

In THE NEWGATE CALENDAR, where—among the bigamists and adulterers, Wakefield, kidnapper of *maidens*—is also to be found Ann Marrow, pilloried in 1777 for pretending to be a man, marrying three women, and in this way taking money and valuables from them. The contempt of the crowd, it says in the calendar, in particular the contempt of the female members of the crowd, is so great that Marrow is pilloried (presumably with stones and rubbish) violently enough that she permanently loses her eyesight.

—

My awkward remarks when someone asks me on the street outside Mars Bar what I'm working on:

THE CONQUEST OF NATURE OR THE VIRGIN
THE FORCIBLE PENETRATION INTO NEW
TERRITORIES (OVERSEAS)
HUNGER AS CONSTITUTION
LOVE etc.

—

Last night I was drafting another message to C.—I say to A.—but I kept falling asleep at it, and when I woke up hours later, it was already light. I lay at the window and watched how the snow pushed by the wind rushed toward me at high speed, as if the flakes were silently assaulting me, as if they were all bearers of one and the same message that they were going to repeat urgently until at last I deciphered it.

—

How Don Diego de Zama, royal official in the service of the Spanish Empire, contemplates nature in the Asunción area according to Benedetto in 1790: Gentle—he says—and childlike; he runs the risk of being captured by Nature and brought to deceptive, long-echoing thoughts, especially in those moments of languor when he is just barely awake.

—

At that moment—I say to A.—looking out this morning at the neighboring house and the snow-covered fields, I thought about nature—about nature, its discoverers and subjugators, about nature as woman, about woman between man and nature—and I realized that I have to abandon the quail and the tropical tortoises, those old-fashioned images of a humid and sultry wilderness; that I cannot fall back on them to describe to C. the place to which I want to lure him.

How about Brinkmann's *southern construction* instead, A. suggests. Or—I say—I know how to access the deep Web, I write my own Transmission Control Protocol now, I choose random routes, pass through portals without logging my data; I have my own servers, I am a user with myriad names: I am a U.S. Air Force Master Sgt. from Wyoming with sad gray eyes, I am an animal, just an animal coming, I'm *so hrny*, user name *Pastor_ Ryan*, female, age 28, from Bexley GB, my tits are so beautiful, I'll get naked if I feel like it for a random string of letters, move around without a problem on the wide field of discrete structures,

because my mother could code ("Derevaun Seraun!"),

I want the private crypto key to caps lock EVERY-THING.

—

Mr. Carr, what are you? – A coachmaker.

Where? – Manchester.

Do you recollect two gentlemen coming to your workshop on the 6th of March, on a Monday morning? – Yes.

Who were they? Do you see them now–do you see the gentlemen? – Yes.

Mr. Edward Wakefield? – Yes.

Did Mr. William Wakefield come with him? – Yes. [...]

Now, did Mr. Edward Wakefield say anything to you? – Yes.

What did he say? – He said he wanted to purchase a used carriage.

What time of day was it? – A little after ten in the morning.

Mr. Edward Wakefield said he wanted to buy a used carriage? – Yes.

Did he ask if you had one? – Yes.

Did you show him one? – Yes.

Now, what color was it? – Green.

Dark-green or light-green? – A darkish green.

(*Trial of the Wakefields*, Evidence of Mr. William Carr.)

Did Miss Turner get into the carriage? – She did.

Did she remark anything about the carriage? – Yes, she said it was not her papa's carriage.

(*Trial of the Wakefields*, Evidence of Miss Elizabeth Daulby.)

—

I race through England in a carriage, I hear the sound
of the horses' shod hooves hurrying through the night,
see the back of the French coachman on his seat. I open
my coat, then my jeans, and run my hand between my
legs into the warmth, to the warm origin of the world,
as a painter whose work I studied extensively called it;
it grows quite pleasurable, I egg myself on, whip myself
up, goad myself, watch as it all comes to crisis; I let
myself go, through all of England I let myself go, and
everything we pass is mine—the houses and the streets;
the automobiles and the animals; the neon lights on the
façades of the main streets; the playhouses, fruit stands,
and cake shops of the country; the outgoing ships; the
great oceans—I give myself everything, can give myself everything now, everything is a subject to me, but
especially the Frenchman who guides the horses, my
little French servant, even though I'm only 15, what did
you think?

In two years, I'll marry a rich neighbor. And in four
years I'll be dead.

New World Plaza

Yesterday at the cinema, in Éric Rohmer's film *La Collectionneuse*: Haydée Politoff throwing stones at the chickens.

Home through pouring rain.

—

With C. on the balcony, a Sunday afternoon, nothing happening, no one moving, only the February sun slowly setting. We drink wine from thin-walled glasses. Once we're sitting in the shade, over C.'s right shoulder the windows of the houses on the Hönggerberg shine gold in the evening light.

I read an entry in Wolfram that immediately jumps out at me as a wildly appropriate description of this document and my poking around in it.

S. 676:
Hyper U, with shopping list

I'm always running back and forth, been at it for over an hour

Where is sugar, I can't find it
Sugar!

Especially because I started with sugar—with the sugar eater in Akerman, the Caribbean sugarcane fields, with Adam Smith's fingers in the sugar bowl, and now I'm slowly making my way back to it.

—

When I get home at noon, I see that the elevator is stuck, and on my floor: the doors are half open, and inside the light is still on, but the floor of the car is about half a meter lower than the hallway in front of it. Immediately I have the nonsensical thought that I came home late and drunk the previous night and pried open the elevator doors from the inside with the surprising strength of drunk people, then climbed out of the elevator through the gap.

Similarly: remembering something I did three or four days ago, constantly accompanied by the feeling that it was not I but another person who was the protagonist of that action—a woman watching a documentary film about the avalanche winter of 1999 at two in the morning; a person in a black coat waiting in the foyer of the Schauspielhaus; a person driving onto the Duttweiler Bridge shortly after 11 p.m.

This confusion that writing foments instead of providing clarity: That's why the elevator stops half a meter below. As I clamber out with a groan, I see out of the corner of my eye what's under the floorboards, what lies between floors.

Who is this madwoman anyway, climbing out of the elevator with a threadbare cape around her shoulders?

The empty elevator at night, the doors open a crack; inside, the light illuminates its backdrop-like, matte-green walls:

The scene of my nocturnal escapades.

—

How I carved my initials into the red wall next to the elevator with my mailbox key. I was already thirty years old at the time.

—

In the folder of "sugar" notes I'm reviewing today, on a piece of graph paper lying among other sheets of key words about sugar beets, sucrose, and the Caribbean plantations, my handwritten note:
Lotto king was v. thin

Only after a while do I understand that this statement could not have been only about the physique of the lottery king; with my note I probably wanted to remember that the fact of his thinness might have indicated some form of starvation or destitution.

Thin, tall,
  light, cool eyes.

—

One picture shows him—Werner Bruni, lotto winner—
kneeling in front of a sink, a toilet in the background.
He is wearing work clothes, his hair combed back; on
the tile in front of him lies a pair of pliers.

Parts of his body are brightly illuminated as if light
were falling through a small window very high up to his
right, the kind of pooling light that can be observed in
chapels, for example.

In his hands a white, Y-shaped drain pipe.

—

Werner Bruni (*The Terrible, Sudden Freedom*, April 9,
1980):

– You told me that you don't go to restaurants anymore.—Yes, at least not like before. It's not interesting
anymore. The workers you used to sit with, you can't,
you can't talk to them anymore, it's just… They always
look at you like a black sheep.
– So you lost friends and acquaintances by winning the
lottery?—Yes, a good number of them, yes.

—

On the screen, the mouth of the lottery player, which slowly opens and closes. I can't think of anything to say, nothing at all, instead I drink the white wine that's in the fridge.

—

I remember someone talking about the *theater of war* some time ago; it might have been A. who said that as recently as the nineteenth century, the theaters of war in the world were actually called "theaters," just as the great complexes and auditoriums of nature were called "sceneries," illuminated for a moment by an eternally returning sun and then left behind again.

—

My own, smallest theater of nature and war and the world in general has shown only one scene for several years, in an extreme expansion of time: the auction of two figures made of ebony or some black stone for thirty-five francs in the hall of an inn on the southern shore of the Thunersee.

The main character of the play, the gambler and laborer B., whom the lottery commission crowned "king" six years earlier, does not make an appearance. It is his absence that fuels the scene: the extras have flocked to celebrate the fall of the one who owed his rise from their circle to but a few luckily chosen numbers: 11, 40, 29, 2, 33, 15, bonus number 31.

As if I can't leave the dark auditorium of this theater until I achieve, on these pages, narrating, some form of redemption. Or so it now seems to me sometimes.

The deafening screech of the half-dead, the undead.

—

– But is the claim that you are simply incapable of doing what is commonly understood as "storytelling" false?
– No, that is correct.
– What's stopping you?
– Well, it's just that every possible thing happens while I'm sitting at my desk. I can hear the voices of people in the hall returning from lunch; outside there's a double-decker Intercity train leaving the city; people in orange vests are walking around with folding rulers on the roof of the building next door; and someone sends me a message from Antigua, Guatemala, and of course all of this has to be told, because these are the conditions under which the text is created, the circumstances in which I write. But it is quite impossible for me to bring these things into the text in their simultaneity.
– But the way you're saying it now in this rundown, I do hear it as something simultaneous.
– The way I'm saying it now, I don't like. I consider it a lack of style when I read something like that in a text.

I put, for example, the same sentence on paper over and over for months, saying that I'm standing in a parking lot on the American East Coast eating bánh da lợn. So, "I'm standing in a parking lot," and so on. And with that, of course, I wanted to say that someone is standing there eating, yes, and at the same time, of course, the "American parking lot," we know that from the movies, seen it a thousand times, and then the "American East Coast"—so big, that immediately opens everything up, this forever-long stretch of coastline and before it, the ocean. But it also closes some things down, if you think about current politics or, again, certain movies or books that are so boring. Those things are perhaps in there, in the sentence. But at the same time, I also thought of it against the background or with a footnote by Merleau-Ponty from the '40s, where he writes that the word "here," when applied to one's own body, is not a determination of place in relation to other places where the body has also been or to other coordinates. Rather, the word "here" in this sense always designates the "determination of first coordinates." So at the same time, my sentence should say HERE in this way, HERE it starts, and also doubt this HERE at the same time, because it's just a sentence in literature that I wrote, and the body of the I that says HERE is therefore a fiction, an assertion. In addition, the talk of "first coordinates" gains a second meaning in this parking lot, located in the so-called New World, where I immediately see Columbus standing there between the cars in his colorful, ridiculous uniform eating a roll. Recently, when I looked at this strip mall again on the Internet—and I think this is ridiculous—I saw that there is a sign saying "New World Plaza."

Yes, and then it occurs to me in relation to Merleau-Ponty that Iris Marion Young wrote in "Throwing Like a Girl" that the woman—woman in quotation marks, I think, "woman"—experiences herself as "inserted into space." Her body is a "thing like other things in the world," a "thing that exists by *being looked at*." So, a declaration that says, for a woman—whatever that's supposed to mean—these first coordinates do not exist in the same way, or better: the first coordinates do not coincide with her body, because she always sees herself from the outside as well. What does that mean if it's true now, and birds fly by, and then dusk comes, what kind of feeling is that now and so on?

– One could also say that this is complete overkill—an unreasonable demand, really.

– Right. These sentences, I have to understand, will never achieve any kind of pure, radiant clarity, ridding themselves of all additional and confused meanings. They are actually more flickering, difficult constructions, I think, dark whirlpools in which everything, including everything peripheral, swirls with deafening noise forever around an unstable center. And more is always being pulled in.

—

So I'm standing in a parking lot on the U.S. East Coast eating *bánh da lợn*. (March 2016)

Next to me is a blue Honda Accord; on the car roof the steamed cake; in my luggage the folder labeled "sugar." Dusk. A few miles away, the Delaware River flows under mighty bridges toward the Atlantic. The river widens toward its mouth, the flat terrain near the coast becomes a staging area for northward migrating night herons and sandpipers, the Atlantic migratory route of snow geese passes these marshes, thousands of horse-shoe crabs appear on shore in cycles.

The light is now receding in a westerly direction, leaving the Atlantic Ocean, this historic corridor, in a dark pool of night. At its edge lie artificially lit metropolises, port cities, uninhabited summer homes. Passenger planes leave the airports of the East Coast for Europe in short intervals.

Inside the car the display of a telephone lights up; outside: PHỞ HÀ, New World Vision Center Contacts & Eyeglasses, 1 HOUR PHOTO, Video & Music, Washington Pharmacy: Lottery – Cigarette – ATM

At the time, I don't know that the parking lot I'm standing in is called NEW WORLD PLAZA.

—

In half-sleep, strange recapitulations: One sun rising over the Greater Antilles; one now at its zenith over West African metropolises; one retreating from Isfahan, from Hyderabad; one still briefly illuminating the trees in the parks of Tokyo Prefecture. I see us standing in a parking lot at dusk, the car doors open; I see the continuing dawn on a transatlantic flight, a hand passes me an orange juice; I see us over and over, first in the light and then in the dark.

—

– It's actually uncomfortable for me to get so far into the personal side of things now. But I'm always involved in everything anyway; or, put another way, that I can never get away from myself is a fact, and I can tell you an anecdote in this context that seems to me to be pretty revealing, at least in retrospect.

– Good.

– It's also one of those stories that, once you tell it, you don't entirely believe yourself. Although it's definitely quite banal.

– That's also fine.

– So I walked through the basement of the main station a few weeks ago without even wanting to take a train. I had come from Central Station and walked through the underpass so as not to have to wait at the traffic lights for so long. I was also very hungry, so I bought a ham sandwich there in the basement. And then, in front of Barth Books, which I frequently visit, I unexpectedly met the director of the archive that handles Max Frisch's estate.

– Do you know each other?

– From college, though it was over ten years ago now that we were frequently in and out of the same institute building; we sometimes smoked cigarettes together on Leipzig's Demmeringstraße, right where it curves around before it hits Lindenauer Markt. I didn't sleep much back then: in the evenings I went to pubs or to the parties of friends of friends — people I didn't know. I remember sometimes riding my bike home and weaving because I was drunk off my ass, and falling asleep on the cold floor next to the toilet. And you know that the house where I lived then was still heated with coal, and the toilet was halfway up a set of stairs, somebody had built it in the former pantry, which was a small room that faced the kitchen like a kind of bay window, so it was very exposed and very cold in the winter, and I remember very well how it felt to wake up there, the whole surface of my body very cool.

In any case, I didn't see him again for years after that, until he took up his post as director; I read about it in the newspapers then, and acquaintances from Germany had also told me about it.

We greeted each other, and he asked pretty directly what I was currently working on, and without thinking I said—though it wasn't at all true—the manuscript I was working on had the working title *Montauk 2*. I'm interested in the question, I said—and you have to imagine that I'm still standing there with the ham sandwich in my hand in front of the bookstore display window with crowds and train travelers walking by with their luggage and shopping bags, pushing me inch by inch in the director's direction—so I said that I was interested in what Frisch's *native form* could be in my case, the *native form* that he claims to reveal in his American story, if one takes seriously the motto he uses to preface his book.

– I don't remember that.

– It's a passage from Montaigne's preface to his *Essais,* and it says that it is "a well-meaning book" in which the reader can find the author's failings and his "native form, so far as respect for social convention allows." Frisch skips the sentence that directly follows this passage, by the way, and concludes with God and the date, March 1, 1580. The sentence that Frisch omits actually refers to this *native form,* because it reads: "For had I found myself among those people who are said still to

89

live under the sweet liberty of Nature's primal laws, I can assure you I would most willingly have portrayed myself whole, and wholly naked."

So there I stood, and the director eyed me and the bread I was holding in my left hand. I was really hungry, but I waited, very controlled; he eyed me with an expression of mild surprise, then he smiled kindly; he's without question a very friendly person, and he said, while already slowly moving away, that the archive was of course open to me at any time.

– That's the whole story?

– Yes.

– You said earlier that this anecdote might be revealing.

– Yes, well, of course I think it's obvious. You know I've never thought it advisable to have myself appear directly in a text, and that still applies, and yet there I stand with the ham sandwich. And it doesn't matter in principle whether the sandwich actually existed or not, etc. etc., to be honest, the whole story didn't go down like that, but in my mind at least it very often happens that I'm standing somewhere and have the feeling that at the most inappropriate moments I'm holding a similar sandwich in my hand. It doesn't even have to be a sandwich, it could be a bucket filled with a cloudy liquid. Or this: I own a jacket, a very beautiful jacket in my opinion. I bought it ten years ago in a department store at Frankfurter Tor, and since then I've worn it every winter, and although it wasn't at all expensive — because I couldn't have afforded that at the time, an expensive coat — it's still very beautiful, but the lining is torn on the inside in a lot of places and the insulation is bulging out and dirty and matted somehow. So it could also be that I'm just standing there in my jacket with the tattered lining, out of place somehow, not native etc.— that would be the same thing.

What I want to say is I take it all very personally. Because the situation is always this: I think about things and go to the library, but the questions come to me physically at the same time, in front of the window displays in the train station underpass, etc.

—

Night after night I stand in that parking lot in Philadelphia and eat steamed cake; it's March, and the evenings are still cool. From the car, soft music can be heard; the man at the wheel, a young American, adjusts the rearview mirror, starts the engine. Later: wharves, abandoned industrial area, feeder roads, the routinized movements of the American's hands on the wheel; in my lap I hold the plastic cake container.

—

– As I sat at the gate in Newark on the way back to Europe, I could only see—for a long time and in a kind of infinite loop, so to speak—the hands of the young American (F.) at the wheel, or how they carefully buttoned his shirt up to the top button, or when he had just returned from the swimming pool and threw the car keys and the mail on the living room table as he entered the room, an optician's bill, a Marxist magazine or something like that, advertising brochures. How, as he spoke, he ran his hand over his right upper thigh, how his fingers followed the line of the muscle down to his knee.

The day after my return, I visited an exhibition of archaeological finds with my sister. You know that my sister is an archaeologist?

– Yes.

– The rooms were dark, and in the vitrines were shimmering green glass vessels and small, bright arrowheads, brooches, and charred grains of grain, also a needle — an accidental find, as it is called, that had been made during an excavation in Sarganserland. My sister had been there herself; she had worked on that site for several weeks, and she was really happy to see this needle, which was perhaps five centimeters long and covered with a sophisticated pattern.

– Can you get excited about archaeology?

– I can't even imagine a job like that, standing outside day after day in the open fields next to the railroad tracks or on the site of a proposed shopping center in the midlands, digging. But my sister, she can drive an excavator, and that's got to be pleasurable. So I also think it's great that she does that.

Then we were standing in front of the vitrines, and I observed the carefully crafted artifacts for a long time, but I didn't see anything, just kind of textured surfaces, and really all I had in mind were those hands. I didn't say a word. I could never speak the names of those I desired or loved in front of friends: it was as if I were exposing everything at that moment, turning myself inside out completely, revealing everything, because I associated such a tremendous feeling with those names. My friends, as you know, still speak today of "the

American," "the movie goer," "Goldilocks," and "the writer," and so on.

—

How I sit back then in the passenger seat of the moving car: The light of the streetlights grazes me at regular intervals, on my knees the cake container.

A few months or maybe a year later in a book by Susan Buck-Morss, I read Adam Smith's biographer John Rae's description from *Life of Adam Smith*, p. 338: The economist once took sugar cube after sugar cube from a bowl at tea without even sitting down at the table, until the hostess, an elderly lady, at last had no choice but to take the bowl "on her own knees," in order to save the sugar from Smith's "uneconomic grasp."

Life of Adam Smith, chapter XXI ("In Edinburgh"): Soon after Smith settled in Edinburgh in 1778, he founded a weekly *dining club*, the "Oyster Club," with Black, a chemist, and Hutton, a geologist. You could not have found three men, Rae writes, who would make less of the *pleasures of the table* than those three fathers of modern chemistry, modern geology, and modern economics. Hutton was a teetotaler; Black, a vegetarian, who usually took only bread, some prunes, and milk diluted with water. Smith himself had only one weakness: *lump sugar.*

On the evening in question—according to Rae—Smith does not comply with the request to sit down at the *tea-table*. Instead, he continues to walk around the table, stopping only occasionally to steal a piece of sugar from the *sugar basin*, the bowl that the elderly spinster finally takes to her knees in order to protect the sugar—*the eternal sugar*—from him.

Rae: This is probably a variant of the story Chambers tells in *Traditions of Edinburgh*. There it takes place in Smith's own living room, and the woman with the sugar in her lap is not an older unmarried woman, but Smith's cousin, Miss Jean Douglas.

In Susan Buck-Morss: the question of whether Smith's desire for sugar could possibly be understood as "a displacement of Smith's sexual desire for his cousin."

The coincidence of the two objects of desire at that moment when the woman at the table takes the sugar bowl into her custody: the sugar from the Caribbean plantations in the lap of the lady or cousin; the unbridled, excessive consumption of one or the other as the economist's dream.

—

I dream—I say to A.—that F., while placing his right hand on the headrest of the passenger seat and backing out of the parking space, casually relates that twice he came across a quotation from Richard B. Kimball, president of an American railroad company. In 1858, Kimball asked a rhetorical question about the connection between the factories of Manchester and the

American wilderness: Indeed, when he entered the European city, a buzzing sound came to his ears — a great, nonstop vibration, as if there were an unstoppable and mysterious force at work.

And I said to myself, what connection shall there be between Power in Manchester and Nature in America?

—

ETERNAL SUGAR (?)

—

What I don't know when I see F. approaching me for the first time across the NEW WORLD PLAZA: that in this moment his person becomes connected with my research, and therefore everything that follows becomes quite personal.

Back then, without asking, he places himself among the men and women of Spiez, so to speak, who have gathered in the hall on the southern shore of the Thunersee that has been transformed into an auction house in order to view the objects up for auction from the estate of lotto player B.

Precisely for this reason, I think now, I never questioned him about his ancestors, about the men and women linked to him by kinship through past centuries, the course of their lives on the island of Saint-Domingue/Haiti before and after the Revolution: he is not to become part of this research that has long been underway.

No question about his family name, which claims a fantastic French grandeur, as if he came from a dynasty of kings, regents, gods, as if he had lived all his life in palaces and castles, spent his childhood in the Elysian fields.

—

Geggus, p. 275: Very few of the women, men, and children trafficked across the Atlantic to work on the Haut-du-Cap plantation of the Brédas still bore their former West African names—instead, the names of saints, invented first names, names derived from antiquity.

Toussaint Louverture, too, for example: until the Revolution—when he becomes the opening through which the insurgents can pass, when he declares himself the overture of a free future—he, Toussaint, bears the name *Tous-saint de Bréda* after the family that owns him and several sugar plantations on the northern coast of Saint-Domingue.

—

Once, much later, in the car, F. describes the dilapidated Palais Sans Soucis, which King Henry I, a former slave, had built a few years after the Revolution a few kilometers south of the Bréda plantations.

On his bookshelf, C. L. R. James's famous account of
the Haitian Revolution:

PROLOGUE

*Christopher Columbus landed first in the New World at
the island of San Salvador*

         Haiti, a large island

(nearly as large as Ireland)
    He sailed to Haiti.

—

Today, when I pull my own copy from the shelf, I immediately open to the page in the first chapter of the book
where James quotes, from the travelogues of a Swiss
(Girod-Chantrans), the description of a large group of
enslaved men and women at their hard, deadly work on
a sugar plantation.

—

How then to understand this moment when Adam
Smith, instead of indulging his desire for the cousin,
reaches for the sugar made from the sugar cane of the
Caribbean plantations—*affreuses campagnes,* dreadful
country, as Girod-Chantrans writes in 1782 in his fifth
letter from Saint-Domingue, from which he averts a
gaze "imbued with sadness & a kind of horror."

And what does that make of us now, standing next to
the Honda in the twilight, F. and I—I who only have

eyes for him, whom I've long been wanting to offer a piece of the aforementioned cake.

—

Girod-Chantrans, Lettre XXXI. *Sur l'origine des montagnes. S. Domingue 1782*:
"Let us take the globe before its first rotational movement. The waters then spread over its solid part must cover it entirely and present a perfect sphere.
The rotation begins, the equilibrium is broken, and the shape immediately changes."

—

The Philadelphian strip mall parking lot as a point of departure, I say to A., is possibly related to Fichte's small Portuguese town on the Atlantic. A woman is standing in the parking lot eating dessert just as it's getting dark. In Fichte it's "Eu como tudo." I eat everything.

—

For days I sleep badly. C. appears again in my dreams. We are high up in the mountains looking down on the Adriatic, then again in the parking lot in Philadelphia: I am standing on the NEW WORLD PLAZA; the young American is letting the car key spin around his finger; and on the roof of the Honda is the container with the cakes prepared from mung beans, rice flour, and the juice of a tropical screw palm.

I see myself finally handing him a piece of it.

Then I open the car door and get in.

—

A suspension bridge stretching far across the wide body of water before us, its towering piers crowned with red lights.

The *USS Olympia*, F. says overlooking a cruiser docked at the pier. Americans piloted the warship into Manila Bay in May 1898 to fight Spanish colonial power.

Later, the lights of the suburbs grazing our faces. On the dashboard a bag of Pepperidge Farm Goldfish.

—

I know a place, I write to C., from three years ago (NEW WORLD PLAZA), when lucky me didn't waste a thought on you.

—

The sugar eater in Chantal Akerman ("Je, tu, il, elle," 1974):

Et je suis partie, she says, but before she leaves, she removes the furniture from the room, always moving the last remaining mattress and herself into new positions, as if it weren't possible to stay in one place any longer.

On the sixth day, she begins writing letters, and as she writes page after page, she eats finely ground sugar from a brown paper bag.

Je mangeais de temps en temps une grosse cuillerée de sucre en poudre. Occasionally I ate a big spoonful of powdered sugar.

How she once, at night, lies naked in the semi-darkness on the letters scattered on the floor and eats spoonful upon spoonful.

She waits, she says, "until it's over or until something happens, until I believe in God or you send me gloves to go out in the cold."

Her naked, white body reflected in the floor-to-ceiling windows. Soon she will set off on the expressway, finally arriving in town at the home of a woman who spreads Nutella on her sandwiches and pours wine, who allows the buttons of her dress to be opened at the table.

Pleasures of the table.

J'ai su que j'avais faim, I knew I was hungry, says the sugar eater, and when the bag is empty she gets up, dresses herself, and leaves.

—

The European passion for sugar. The white body of the Belgian woman on film. Her desire (1974), a small white mountain of sugar on the floor in front of her mattress.

And Girod-Chantrans, who day and night hears the eerie trembling of the *sucreries* on Saint-Domingue—the noise of the mills and the carts bringing in the harvest, the sound of the whips.

From the furnaces and boiler houses—he writes—the smoke flows in streams that then pour over the land, or rises into the air as dark clouds.

—

– Were you going anywhere in particular that day in Philadelphia?
– No. There was a suggestion to visit the Russian baths.
– The suggestion did not come from you.
– No.
– I have the feeling that nothing would appeal to you about such a place.
– I can't say. This wasn't a simple spa either like you might be familiar with, but a somewhat run-down, sprawling complex, and in the large swimming hall from which tiled corridors led to the various baths and saunas, the bathers—large families, groups—sat on white plastic chairs, drank beer, and ate borscht and olives, also lots of meat, long shashlik skewers, things like that. But it's true that I usually stay out of such places because they can exhaust me, I mean my eyes, they exhaust my eyes.
– Why?
– Because, as I see it, what we usually show with

such reserve, our wholly naked bodies, to paraphrase Montaigne, suddenly become a focus, and that is what I find extremely interesting, because I basically always want to see everything there is, which means all possible forms, all shapes of the body, all stages, all versions, all its deformations. That's why I'm always thrown into a state of extreme tension or nervous attention in these places. And then of course there's one's own body and the feeling of reflecting on one's self physically, too.

– A self-consciousness?

– Which I also find quite understandable in this case.

—

Merleau-Ponty on the "space of the body": This space is in relation to the outside space "like the darkness of the theatre required for the clarity of the performance, the foundation of sleep."

—

And on the so-called "geometral": Imagine, says A., for example, a house in France, not far from the Seine. High up in the air a plane is making its way. This house is always viewed from a certain direction, from a certain perspective; one sees it differently from the bank of the Seine than from the airplane or from its own interior, the interior of the house. But the actual house, the actual house on the bank of the Seine in France — Merleau-Ponty writes — is different from all these hundreds and thousands of views of this house seen from a great height, or from the other bank, or from the inside.

It is "the non-perspective from which all perspectives could be derived"; it is the *geometral* of all possible perspectives, "the house, seen from nowhere."

For days—I say—while wiping the dust from the leaves of the trout begonia—I've woken up suddenly just before eight in the morning, instantly wide awake. If I'm hungry, I eat a piece of bread and small, expensive oranges with leaves still hanging from their stems.

Me as a house, as a geometral, seen from nowhere.

—

In a book Stefan sends me from Vienna, the lines of the poet May Swenson ("Question"):

Body my house
my horse my hound
what will I do
when you are fallen

Where will I sleep
How will I ride
What will I hunt

[...]

—

How I once, at night, lay naked on the floor in the semi-darkness, a spoon in my mouth.

—

On January 23, I drive to the Kleine Wannsee and look for the place where Henriette Vogel let herself be shot by Kleist in the left breast and through the heart in November 1811. It starts to rain even before I cross the B1. The boats of the water sports community have been brought ashore for the winter and covered with white tarpaulins. Leafless woody plants, evergreen creepers; beyond that everything is gray.

"Some mud.
Concrete." (Fichte)

They called him "Vogel's house friend"—I say to A.—"and when asked if they wanted to eat something for lunch, they replied that they would just drink some broth and eat all the better that evening."

On the way there, I say to A., I thought once again: My native form as a woman, what's that? The woman, seen from nowhere? The woman as a young man in Paris, who pulls a splinter out of his foot?

Maybe—says A.—like this: A friend told him about how now and then large, hooded crows land on the windowsill of her study. Recently, she watched the birds from her desk for a while, then suddenly and to her own surprise, she threw both arms up in the air like a woman possessed and watched the crows fly away, laughing loudly.

On the same day, between the branches of the forest pines the silvery gray of the Schlachtensee, a young couple takes the path toward the shore. I remembered, I say, the trunks colored red in the evening light, the broad umbrella crowns of the pines in a painting by Leistikov.

—

The Russian Baths of Philadelphia: a low-rise building in the northern foothills of the city, a heavily heated and aging temporary structure with thin walls.

Walking through the tiled hallways and the warm, humid rooms of the building. From a distance, the sound of water sloshing over the edge of a pool. In the hall are the many bodies, their details and structures; the simple or complex shapes; their pigmentation; signs of age, loss, injury, abundance and pleasure; thighs, torsos, private parts.

Children slithering across the tiles in bath sandals and dropping themselves into the water in a careless, extravagant manner.

—

At the edge of the pool, I say to A., F. is sitting in a bathrobe on a plastic chair, reading the *New York Review of Books*. Above his head is the suggestion of a balustrade, copies of antique sculptures: white bodies, slender shackles, artfully braided hair.

Later we open a door, take off our bathrobes, and enter the low room. The heat reduces the space; it wraps around the body like a leaden, pleasantly weighty cloak. The heat, it captures us. We sit opposite each other on wooden benches; far above us towers an old man breathing heavily, a cap of golden felt pulled low on his forehead.

—

Dream: In the NEW WORLD PLAZA Heinrich von Kleist stands and writes a novella (*The Betrothal in Santo Domingo*).

In the news today, they say a sixteen-year-old teenager fell from the eighth deck of the cruise ship *Harmony of the Seas* as it was anchored in the port of Labadee on the northern coast of Haiti.

—

The woman who is me is tortured by the heat in the Russian bathhouse. Crossing her arms in front of her body, she has a vision of a divan in a cool chamber: she wants to lie asleep under blankets, and F. would enter the room, put the car key on the living room table, sit down, and read an essay about commodity fetishism's inversion of social relations.

And the next moment—I say to A.—*La Blanche* is lying on the divan again as Vallotton painted her in 1913, naked and pale, her cheeks flushed, and next to her,

106

smoking, *La Noire*. I can't get over it: what all don't we inherit and learn and repeat, the things we know, and the things we want to see differently, and finally want to do differently—to see a thigh, for example, only as such, as a thigh. But as we enter those Russian baths, I am struck by the ancient statues, as I saw them as a child in a hot summer in Greece on the way from Patras to Kalamata, and there we sit in the heat, fittingly unclothed, referred back to our bodies, which are our very own bodies and at the same time revealing ambassadors, indiscreet emissaries of history. There we sit, *la Blanche* and *le Noir,* and on the steps around us are our ancestors from the Old and the New Worlds, there the European *overseas* entrepreneur, the Pineapple King, ship crews, slave drivers, gamblers, and sugar addicts, and there are those who were sold for 300 pounds of cowry money, former inhabitants of the West African kingdoms, African aristocrats, those who survived the Middle Passage, who stood in the deadly sugar cane fields, who made a hole, an opening in history and, as revolutionaries, discarded the names of their masters, their owners.

There we sit, listening to the deafening noise of the *sucreries* at night.

—

When I then see him again, F., after a few months, I pull a book I also own from his shelf (*Sweetness and Power: The Place of Sugar in Modern History*). As a frontispiece is an engraving by William Blake from

1796: Africa, Europe, and America as unclothed women (Black, White, and Native American, respectively) clasping each other's shoulders and hands, almost sisterly. Only the golden rings that Africa and America wear around their upper arms identify them as slaves of Europe: *Europe Supported by Africa and America*.

Above it is a quote from Bernardin de Saint-Pierre's VOYAGE A L'ISLE DE FRANCE, A L'ISLE DE BOURBON, AU CAP DE BONNE-ESPERANCE, &c:
"I don't know if coffee and sugar are necessary for the happiness of Europe, but I do know that these two plants have brought misfortune to two parts of the world. We depopulated America in order to have a land to plant them: we depopulate Africa in order to have a nation to cultivate them."

—

How quickly the clouds move toward the north this morning, multi-story opaque buildings, their roofs and domes illuminated.

At night C. spreads out before my eyes again as a sunlit landscape—a landscape that has always been lost: the memory of a promise.

Standing at the window all morning listening to music.

You are made of sugar, you are sweet

Bellevue 2

Tonight, a dancer with fluttering hands and fearfully swinging, flapping arms on stage at the Opera House: Vaslav Nijinsky, who dances or is being danced, brought up once again from the sanatoriums of the early twentieth century, where he supposedly still sits and just looks, sadly, as an airplane flies through the sky high above him.

Dances as if his eyes had been propped open with matches,

the restless dance of the undead.

Upstairs in the balcony, pretty close to the painted ceiling, next to me is C., for whom everything is much too narrow,

bent *poplar tree by the water-rich river*, uncomplaining.

I am in his immediate environment, so close that I can perceive the incessant, fine movements of his body that indicate a person is alive, that this man next to me is, as they say, *alive*, and I would only need to raise my hand to touch him, his knee or whatever.

The light, almost translucent skin under his eye.

The dancer on stage is about to sit down; his body is already performing all the movements required for this, and I watch him do so with a feeling of relief: I wish

him, the sweating dancer, this restless embodiment of
Nijinsky, recovery, redemption,

as I also hope for redemption for myself, a minor
redemption, which would be that my hand might finally
overcome the distance that remains and come to rest
somewhere there,

but at the last moment the man on stage straightens
again and continues with his fearsome, nervous dance.

Later when we step outside it's raining. The surface
of the square we cross toward the streetcar stop called
Bellevue all black and shiny, as if we were walking
over deep waters.

—

One of the British Royal Mail Steam Packet Company's
ocean liners — all of which are named for rivers, *Amazon*,
Aragon, *Araguaya*—underway on the South American
route, from Southampton to Buenos Aires.

I see it from far off, the big white craft (*new twin-screw,
11,073 tons*) as a small thing under a gigantic, truly immense blue sky in August 1913.

The day after the ship weighs anchor in Southampton,
Nijinsky boards it on the north coast of France: the "Ballets
Russes" are on their way across the Atlantic for a tour of
South America. They are traveling without the director of
the company, who is Njinsky's lover: he, Djagilew, fears,
as the texts say, he won't survive the ship's passage, that
days-long journey into the radiant blue.

—

At the bar in the Café Odeon, someone wants to tell us how short life is—very short, a few centimeters between thumb and index finger, he illustrates.

His name is Martin.

Behind us the streetcars stop at Bellevue, wait there in the rain for a while with the doors open, and then leave again: small, warmly lit capsules.

C. eats peanuts.

Since I saw that light, I think—the light of the apparition when C. appeared, that glare that made me reflexively go down on my knees, arms folded protectively in front of my face, like the sick in the Holy District of Lourdes—all things show themselves to me again as they did when I was very young: every place, every room, every person as an opportunity for intimate acts, uncoordinated dances, hasty unions.

Only this time I seem to see how inexorably we race toward the end at the same time.

Of the seeing eye.

How short the time I have to see everything there is.

In twenty-seven years you can give your stuff to the literary archive, Lucas said recently as we drank beer in Bern.

And while the candles in the Lourdes grotto slowly burn down, I stand among the last pilgrims and pour holy water from canisters into myself by the liter.

—

Onboard the white ship that August is also a twenty-two-year-old woman, says the dramaturge of the opera house. As she will later write, "twenty-one days of sea and sky" lie ahead of her: twenty-one days on the open ocean to "reform" Nijinsky, the famous dancer without whom she believes she cannot live, the man for whom she long ago decided on for herself.

It is only for this reason that she, Romola de Pulszky, bought a ticket for the passage on the *S. S. Avon*.

In her cabin, next to the bed, hangs a picture of the *Miraculous Infant Jesus of Prague*, the Prague infant Jesus, long believed to have belonged at one time to the holy Teresa of Ávila. At night, kneeling, she asks for his assistance in the Nijinsky case.

There's disquiet in the literature in the fact that during their days together at sea she actually manages to get the dancer to go with her to the registry office in Sección 13 and then to the church of San Miguel Arcángel four days after the ship arrives in Buenos Aires.

References to her wealth, her cool calculation, and her famous mother, to the excessive desire of the reckless admirer who tempts the defenseless Nijinsky aboard the ocean liner and then snatches him away from the world of dance.

As if they all wrote as abandoned lovers, as disappointed lovers.

And maybe they're right, I can't tell.

"In any case, she did not make a good impression at the Bellevue Sanatorium." Max Müller, *Memories*, p. 178.

—

Two o'clock in the morning in the Express Shop on the corner of Militärstraße and Langstraße. Amid the shelves, Peter—unsteady with flitting eyes, his arms and hands flying about, beer cans in his jacket pockets—has no money, no money, nothing.

He is on his way to a place where everything swirls fast, I say to C., or he has been there for a while, in the fast-swirling districts.

C., with a hot dog in each hand, prepared by the man who puts sausages in buns all night long, always, here in the Express Shop.

Peter throws his arms around me, let's get out of here, yes—he says—we'll go where it's warm where we're treated well where milk and honey flow from clay jugs directly into our mouths where everything whirls fast heaven come come yes

High-school students smoking at the bus stop, waiting for the night bus to Bellevue.

—

Five days later, Peter at a bar in Lagerstraße. He had a fight with some idiot on the way here, he says.

What a spectacle!

Lately, he's been thinking a lot about *Synchronicity*.

What a dumbass.

Natalie gets up to refill our glasses at the bar.

Port-au-Prince

Upon my arrival in Philadelphia at the house where F. still lived with friends, I am given a bed in a small room or a kind of walk-in closet, a room that they collectively use as storage for all kinds of things. I sleep between backpacks and dumbbells, hiking boots and the damaged parts of a hi-fi stereo system.

After having filed my notes and photocopies in the "sugar" folder for a long time, thinking that I could follow the events, the persons and their desires, their lapses, without bringing myself into play—in this room I understand that this has always been a misunderstanding.

Lying there among the scattered things of others is my body, deeply involved in everything that happens and that I previously filed away as material.

—

F. stands among the women and men of Spiez, buttoning the top buttons of his shirt while the auctioneer grasps around the waist the two small figures of dark wood or polished stone to present them to the people.

As naturally as he, F., mingles with those present, over time others join them, ancestors, distant relatives, forgotten descendants, as a community of heirs, to complete or challenge the group picture of 1986 with their appearance.

—

In addition, through our liaison, I also got involved with this inn and this text, and now I'm also standing there in the middle of the room, having to watch myself try to explain myself, embarrassed:

I'm here because my eyes were once again bigger than my stomach.

No, strike that.
I was, as always, very hungry.

Hello, yes, you guessed it: I'm a writer. Here you can see my pencil, which I'm always using to write everything down.

—

The sun shines down into the Allgäu, Hinterstaufen, Knechtenhofen, Salmas, all bright and beautiful, snow still on the slopes.
   I'm standing in the train toilet, soap on my hands, but then no water comes, just two tiny drops. Staggering back through the carriage, the smell of the pink liquid soap is everywhere. But the sun says it's all right.

Green Allgäu lake, whose name I don't know. Allgäu paddocks and Allgäu fish farms and Allgäu tree stumps, white from last winter.

In the newspaper, Prince Charles laughing as he turns a big red wheel in Cuba: He's grinding sugar cane. Palm trees.

—

Martin, my editor, says that in case of publication of these notes, "novel" must appear on the cover.

We drive through Munich in a small white car.

I say that it is a report about research, which is why "research report" seems incomparably more appropriate to me.

In Fichte's case, it was also called a "research report."

In the evening, he takes me back to the Central Bus Station, where the buses leave for Mostar, Lyon, and Hamburg.

Then the Allgäu horses on the edge of the highway in the darkness, the edges of Austria, the quiet shores of Lake Constance in the Rhine Valley around 1 a.m.

—

Woke up with the feeling of having long odysseys behind me, of having pulled all-nighters, drunk all-nighters. As if I live a double life whose two realities are bound

together only by this body of mine, the body that partic-
ipates in everything,

day and night,

my house / my horse my dog

—

In the dream I see myself lying asleep amid this junk,
absorbed in the remains of other lives, mouth slightly
open, hair falling over my face.

—

– I knew about the lottery from my grandfather, who
was employed as a foreman at Schindler Elevators, Inc.
and played regularly, mostly by using the birthdays of
his children — i.e., my father, my two uncles and my
aunt — my grandmother and also his own.

– Did he have much luck as a gambler?

– I can't remember any winnings, surely he got smaller
amounts now and then, as often happens.

– Was it something he talked about?

– You have to imagine how my grandparents' life was
dominated by routine, by rituals; at least that's how I
perceived it as a child. There was breakfast, jam on
bread and coffee, then my grandfather's work, which
seemed to me to be so completely removed from our
normal life that as a child, I could not form a concept of
what that work consisted of, or even what it could be,
the work of my grandfather. At most, I thought of it as
an absence, as a daily time of absence. And that only
changed, I would say, when a man with a tie appeared

at my grandfather's grave. With a tie that was some-how not quite right, which immediately marked him as something I could not name, until he introduced himself there, at my grandparents' grave, as someone who had worked with my grandfather at Schindler Elevators, Inc. And—I was twenty then, I think—I understood for the first time that my grandfather had gone to this company every day and worked there and so on... Where was I?

– You were talking about the routines of everyday life.

– So there were the breakfasts, work, lunch, and dinner and in between the walk to the grave of my uncle who died young, then to the WARO supermarket, and to the pond, where we fed the ducks bread—usually in that order. On Sundays they sometimes went to push beds: my grandparents took the sick in the hospital from their rooms on the various ward and floors and rolled their beds into the room where Sunday service was held. Finally, at dinnertime, they would sit in the parlor, a room that was usually locked; they would sit on the up-holstered furniture and watch the news on the television; Grandmother would turn to needlework in the light of the floor lamp, crocheting white doilies as coasters; and I, when I visited, would drink hot chocolate.

The lottery was just another event, one of numerous repetitive actions that in their sum made up the days. I don't know whether it filled my grandfather with excite-ment, waiting for the numbers to be drawn, or whether he thought during the day or before going to sleep that yes, there was always the possibility of winning big.

– One would assume that he had hopes associated with it or certain ideas.

– You think that gambling perhaps expresses the hope

for emancipation, for freedom, just turned apolitical? The utopian in the casino, something like that? But maybe it was a small form of waste that the working woman and the petit bourgeois allow themselves? Here: I'm throwing money out the window, even if it's only a few francs, ha.

– Television and gambling, were those the forms of entertainment your grandparents were familiar with?

– Not entirely. My grandfather built a lot—I would say he was basically an engineer; he drew plans for home organs and then executed them, soldering every single pipe himself. He was interested in electronics and aerodynamics, in flying objects, paper airplanes, miniature airplanes, remote-controlled vehicles in general, the railroads, expeditions, shipping and navigation, model ships, bridge building, telecommunications. He owned atlases and the books of the aviation pioneer Mittelholzer, who was born in the town where my grandfather lived. As a child, I always looked at the pictures of his *Flight to Africa*.

– Do you have any memories from it?

– Yes, those photographs of plumes of smoke rising from the surface of a lake, Lake Nyassa. The heavy ear jewelry of the Kikuyu, the "girl from Nyangori near Kisumu," her nakedness. When I say it like that, it all seems so long ago, fortunately.

—

In the cinema watching Hans-Ulrich Schlumpf's *TransAtlantique* (1983): Onboard the liner *Eugenio C.* the passengers play bingo for the last time.

With Kaschnitz (*diaries*):

May 7, 1962: "We passed Gibraltar at 2 a.m."

Then: "In the afternoon, the lottery, bingo, cards with numbers, the ones that get called out you cover with chips, first a row wins, then the whole card. I never win."

In the evening the *Bal d'adieux*.

—

On January 2, 1984, five years after winning the lottery, Werner Bruni boards a plane in Basel-Mulhouse and flies across the Atlantic to Port-au-Prince.

I say this to F., who is an actual person, with whom I stood in a parking lot next to a car and later lay in a room with at the Albatross Motel in Montauk,

but whose actual person I have long since ceased to mean; I have long since reinvented F. for the purposes of these notes, just as I have reinvented the room in Montauk with its clammy, flower-printed curtains too, the tiny, damp bathroom; also the whole Albatross Motel, the parking lot in front of it, the puddles on the roadside, the whole island, America, the sea, the whole vault of heaven.

—

It's not you I'm writing about, I said last night when he called unexpectedly, but I can't leave you out because I was reading *The Betrothal in Santo Domingo* when I first saw you.

The Betrothal in Santo Domingo.
– A terrible book.

If I hadn't said anything, I would have been concealing something: That I was studying the history of that region, that island (Haiti), with which you are connected.

He can't remember the plot—not the Swiss who flees with his relatives, his servants and maids across the night island to get to Port-au-Prince as quickly as possible. It is the time of the revolution.

It's storming and raining as the Swiss man leaves the starving party in a mountain forest and, in search of food, enters the estate of a man whom the Europeans had once abducted from the Gold Coast of Africa across the Atlantic to the plantation near Port-au-Prince.

– Congo Hoango,
a dangerous black man.

Ungrateful, Kleist writes, to his generous master, Guillaume of Villeneuve: Hoango shoots him when the uprisings take over the plantations, then destroys his estate, roams the countryside, kills farmers, travelers, fugitives, "those white dogs, as he called them."

On this night in 1803, he is on his way to supply General Dessalines with gunpowder and lead. In the house is only his companion Babekan and her daughter.

Toni.

The fifteen-year-old illegitimate daughter of a Frenchman, to whom the Swiss believes he will lose his heart that very evening:

"…He might have sworn, except for her complexion, which repelled him, that he had never seen anything more beautiful."

—

The Inkle and Yarico schema (?)

—

The Swiss man explains in *The Betrothal in Santo Domingo* that the now-freed former slaves of the plantations, seized by the "madness of freedom" and because of the mistreatment they had received from their owners, were now taking revenge on all white people. For example: the girl suffering from yellow fever, who seduces her former master to infect him with the disease.

—

At first a common fever seized her, and she hardly moved for several days. With a sweat cloth she wipes her face dry, and sometimes when she wakes up from a period of sleep, the duration of which she cannot determine afterward, she finds herself in a state like drunkenness, which makes it impossible for her to articulate words clearly, or to perform movements precisely or without trembling. As if she were blind, she slowly guides vessels to her mouth to drink. But no one seriously worries about her because she is young, and she herself is not worried.

From where she is lying, she does not see or hear much of what is happening around her, but those who visit her in the course of the days tell her that there is an upheaval going on. Her brother points to the city: it's happening there right now, things of the greatest importance are happening, we've come so far.

These reports brought to the sick find their way into her sleep as translations in the form of images whose origin she does not know: wide valleys as gathering places, priests in their cassocks with blood oozing black and thick from their mouths, children who have silently taken their seats at the tables of their masters, who lie motionless on the beds of their masters with their limbs stretched out, who stand in front of the doors of their masters' houses without moving. Birds fluttering in the darkness singe their wings on sparking signal fires, fall and stagger into the gloom.

She recovers from her fever, her vision clears, and her concept of space and time is restored. She leaves the room in which she has been waiting for recovery and declares to those with whom she speaks that she is back, now she is back. She still moves with a certain restraint, more slowly than before or perhaps more cautiously, as if she must first determine whether her fever visions have been transformed into a reality and in what condition the city has been thrown during her absence.

When the fever overcomes her a second time and forces her to return to the place that she has just quit, she does not dwell on the misfortune that the illness now means, at this historic moment when everything is changing. Instead, in the last nights remaining to her, she seeks out those to whom the fourteen or fifteen years of her life have belonged. As she tries to stanch the blood running from her nose with the sweat cloth, she sees them once again, standing in the cane fields, overseeing production, their eyes roaming over their property, machinery, mules, labor.

So when, just before the end, someone confides to her that the white man on whose plantation she has learned in a few brief years everything there may be to learn about this miserable life unto death, about the perseverance of the body or mind—when she hears that this man is now hiding in a shed from the insurgents, she sends her brother to him.

Perhaps she has him called because she wants to see him again under these changed auspices that make him a doomed man. Maybe she doesn't want to leave without taking him with her, a small, final act in the battle for freedom that is being fought all over the island at this moment.

In the darkness are her feverish eyes; other signs of the disease are not visible. When the white man enters the room behind her brother, breathing nervously and rapidly as if he had been running, she wakes up from the in-between she is already in, leaving everything she saw there again: her mother dressed in the finest fabrics sitting on a chair in the twilight, small branches formed into secret signs, intertwined limbs on a bright beach in the north of the island, a Frenchman vomiting refined sugar, sucreries *at rest all over the country.*

She then perceives more clearly this man who has followed her brother in the foolish hope that it would ensure him safe refuge, with her, who was formerly his property. His breathing is still compressed and rapid, his eyes have not yet fully adjusted to the darkness. Disoriented, he stands in the middle of the room, while behind him at the doorway, her brother, whose body is tensed to its utmost, ready to kill this man at a moment's notice.

While she is still looking at him, the Frenchman stares into the dirt—stripped of all his means of production, his possessions, his power of definition—he seems to belong to an epoch already past. He approaches and bends over her: here she lies, as familiar to him as the horses, the heavy furniture, and the handkerchiefs embroidered with initials he once owned. And when he sees her like this, her complete, living body, it seems to him that therein lies the promise of a final, if brief, redemption, of his rehabilitation: to possess this body, this person completely in his power once again, even if only for a few, brief hours that night.

Maybe she expected him to approach her in this way; in any case, she doesn't try to push him away from her, or she lacks the strength to fight off his open mouth, the weight of his body.

With certainty she knows that at this moment she herself has become a revolutionary, that now, before she departs, the great upheaval is also happening in this room, when he finally presses himself against her breast as if demanding her milk.

—

In truth, she would have been immune to yellow fever:
The disease, I read, mainly affected European troops.

—

Sex at the Albatross Motel in Montauk,
   as if we were lying in the marriage bed of our parents, the elders; as if the whole world had already lain in this bed; as if they had all laid here with each other, rolled around on these sheets, loved one another, seduced and undressed each other, beaten, consumed, united, hurt, reproduced themselves.

Later, F. in the shower.
   I flip through the channels.

Nope, no one here but ourselves.

—

Sex in Kleist as an omission: the Swiss man on the run, fearful, pulls Toni—she seems so graceful to him—onto his lap and asks her about her civil status, her age. And while he is still holding Toni, whose task is actually to seduce and stall the Swiss so that he can later be killed by Hoango, "embracing her slender body," he whispers jokingly in her ear that "perhaps it should be a white man who carries off her favor,"
   and she blushes and lays herself upon his chest lovingly, etc.

She reminds him, he says, of Mariane Congreve, his betrothed, who laid herself in his place under the guillotine in Strasbourg to die for him because of his remarks about the Revolutionary Tribunal. And the Swiss man weeps for Mariane Congreve,
    and Toni cries too.

"What followed, we do not need to report, because it will be clear to everyone who has followed the narrative thus far." (*Betrothal in St. Domingo*, p. 20)

Except that afterward she lies on the bed, apathetic and motionless, and does not seem to hear what he says (that he owns a small property on the banks of the Aare where he will take her, "fields, gardens, meadows, and vineyards") and does not respond to any of his questions; he finally picks her up and carries her to her chamber.

What led him to this act: "a mixture of desire and fear that she instilled in him."

—

How he later, unable to correctly interpret her actions to save him, shoots her in the chest.

The headless Mariane Congreve.
    The blood-smeared Toni.

—

I think we might have talked about it then, at NEW WORLD PLAZA, or maybe later, on the way to Montauk:

That capitalism has always been exquisitely reliant on multiple divisions of the so-called proletariat,

the result is an accumulation of divisions, of un-fortified trenches and furrows that separate those who in principle are on the same side, namely on the side of those who give too much and get too little in return,

a multiplicity of divisions.

—

My embarrassed response when he asks me at night on the way to Montauk what I'm working on:

Eight or nine years ago I saw a scene on TV that I've returned to ever since, one that not only expresses the fact that capital divides and sets against each other those whose labor it exploits, but also shows the mer-cilessness with which those who transgress these gulfs are put in their place, even if the transgression is only temporary.

That scene from 1986, I say, shows the hall of an inn lo-cated on the southern shore of a Swiss lake. Into the low room and corridor that leads to the hall, the local pop-ulation crowds, men and women and their children — their faces at that moment turned to the man who, with outstretched arms, is auctioning off two small figures made of ebony or black stone. At first glance, I say, one might think that the amused laughter of those present stems solely from the way that the auctioneer brandishes these figures, and certainly their laughter is directed to some degree at these bodies and their composition, but above all, I suspect that these peasant women and service workers, unskilled laborers and employees and their sons and daughters, are laughing at love, at the ridiculous love that the former owner of the figurines, the wage laborer and lotto player WB, must have felt for them. I see—I say—his connection to these figures, which had nothing to do with these bodies but was the actual subversion of relations, a disobedience: WB had made a leap across the divide.

Plaisir 2 / Trocadero

– So, what is love, truly? What all do you want to know! I honestly have no idea; I also find that I confuse things all the time or that we confuse the words. So in the broadest sense, I would say maybe a willingness. What do you think?

– An attentiveness, perhaps, that is without intent?

– Which also always means a turning toward things. In France, it occurs to me that I read within a very short time last summer the *passion simple* of a French writer; although, as you know, I don't speak French at all—I was not even able to indicate the breads in the bakery without touching them or had to ask someone on the street about the bus to the coast. I sat in the kitchen of the apartment that the landlady had claimed was located near the medical school, and when I looked out the window, I saw young men circling the small, unadorned church night after night on silent electric motorcycles, wearing sneakers that slithered across the asphalt. So, I was reading this *passion* and was already quite unhappily in love, and this is why, I think, I could understand every word of the book, although in principle it should not have been possible. At the same time I stopped eating and drinking almost entirely because my lack of language skills left me unable to order the things I desired—small oval cheeses with soft centers, shiny green fish freshly caught from the sea, or varieties of pâté.

– I've noticed recently that you're getting thinner and thinner.

– So, what I mean is that love perhaps always means a connection with things—or, let's say, with the world— such that I no longer look at it dispassionately but am very close to it and can suddenly in a mysterious way also understand it, just as I understood this book.

– And is love also sufficient for you, an end or a saturation?

– Of course I can't begin to answer that since we're speaking in such general terms. You say "love," but you mean romantic love or infatuation. The most I can give you is an example. Recently, I went out of town with C.; we walked for a long time and looked at everything and told each other what we saw and pointed out the things that seemed special and beautiful or strange and even disturbing, then sometime in the early evening we reached a park situated on a slope, through which a winding path led, and we sat down on a bench. It was very quiet; two children were playing below us near the entrance gate, and still further down lay the rail- road tracks and the long, straight streets of this city that Marx had referred to in *Capital* as a "single watch man- ufactory." I suddenly felt how tired I was; my whole body was seized with a great fatigue, so I lay down on the bench, and as I lay there like that, I felt the move- ments of his body as he talked and smoked. I saw some birds, pigeons, pushing off from time to time from the branches that jutted into my field of vision, and C.'s hand resting on the back of the bench; perhaps an hour passed like that, and I was very happy.

– But it wasn't enough?

– No. At some point we got up and rode back; we said goodbye on the sidewalk, and I saw, even as I was still riding my bike past the stadium back home... No, even as I was still lying on the bench and looking up in the air, I saw that the ground was about to open up and I was going to fall into the first hellish abyss that came along. Dimly I saw that I would be alone again. "I lived the pleasure as a future pain," it says in the book I read last August in Marseille.

—

Got off at Versailles-Chantiers station on the way to Plaisir and walked to the chateau. The dining room of the king, the king's bed in the morning sun. The *anti-chambres* of the princesses: locks that the visitor must pass through on the way to the innermost room, the actual heart of one or another royal daughter.

—

The German teacher in the car: The inhabitants of the place are called *les Plaisiroises*. She is adorable and jolly, but does not live here herself, in Plaisir, but in a nearby place that is actually much nicer.

—

In the evening I sit in Paris at the same place (Trocadero) where I sat a few months ago with C. and looked down on the Seine. On a cloth spread out on the ground, a man is making a golden ball disappear under three aluminum cups, which he keeps moving around, accompanied by his chanting:

Easy come easy go hello guys I pay double where is the ball no money no honey hello Madame

—

In Hanna Johansen's *Trocadero*, p. 164:
> "Do you know what I want?" I said breathlessly.
> He could not guess.
> "A lot of everything!" I said.
> "How right you are," he said.

—

Later, back to the hotel, a run-down room somewhere in the Latin Quarter with red, scuffed carpet. All night long, noises come through the walls: water seems to flow incessantly through the pipes, hours of maniacal laughter, knocking, as if craftsmen were at work.

I have breakfast in the small room facing the street. On the sugar cubes wrapped in paper in the bowl on the table are images of sculptures from different parts of the world: *Sculpture îles Marquises*, *Sculpture du Nigéria*, *Sculpture Mexique*.

Did you know, I write to C., that the yews in Plaisir are cut into the shape of sugarloaves?

—

A walk through the city. The children playing soccer in the empty pool of the fountain before the Sainte-Trinité, dust clouds, dusty shoes, dusty pants, everything white and bright light like at the seashore.

—

The initial surprise that these notes lead me again and again to the Atlantic, that I basically always find myself in a new port building, on this ship, then that ship, then a third ship: in my excitement I ran around the apartment. Then, when I came across the Atlantic: the Atlantic Passage as an *event* not only in Ellen West, in Eveline, in Toussaint Louverture, in Fichte, Bruni and Nijinsky, in Frisch, etc., and lastly, without even having tried, in the diaries of Marie Luise Kaschnitz and in M. F. K. Fisher's *The Gastronomical Me* — the great accumulation of apparent coincidences began to exhaust me, as if I were standing in front of a slot machine with coins rolling out in a continuous stream.

I now see how simple the explanation is and that coincidence plays no role in it: The routes of the merchant and passenger ships, the intercontinental flights that emerge here, this network of transatlantic relations and interrelationships touches my concern at its innermost core: what has not been carried across this body of water, this rift between continents in the course of time?

    Indian textiles, precious metals, sugar mountains
    doubly free workers and those forcibly abducted
    avant-gardes (explorers, soldiers, dancers)
    itinerant preachers

Utopian women, those from the poorhouse, those
in exile
    lovesick poetesses
    tourists

Montauk

I wake up after midnight and am hungry. I know that I am in a motel room. It must be the year 2016. The yellowish light of the exterior lighting penetrates through a small, frosted glass window set in the door. In the distance is the sound of the Atlantic Ocean. I am wearing a tattered white T-shirt with the inscription "International Institute for Sport." Next to me lies F., who has pulled the blanket up to his chin in his sleep. His breathing is slow and regular, and I watch him as he lies there. Then, suddenly, I perceive a movement out of the corner of my eye: for a fraction of a second, I think I see a figure in the doorway to the bathroom, a body that has broken free from the darkness and taken a step into the room. A cold shiver runs over my skin. I don't dare turn my face toward the bathroom and I remain motionless, as if I were invisible that way, despite my white T-shirt with the old blood stains on the bottom hem.

—

We drove then through the Hamptons in darkness, F. and I, the linen-bound American edition of Frisch's *Montauk* on the back seat of the blue Honda Accord. In the light of a gas station, I read in translation what I already know in the original:

He knows where they are:

MONTAUK

an Indian name; it denotes the northern tip of Long Island, one hundred and ten miles from Manhattan, and he can also name the date:

11.5.1974

The toilet at the back of the gas station facing away from the street is a shack of dark boards.

My eyes slowly adjust to the sparse light. Trash. Soaked paper towels in the sink. My face in the dirty mirror only a shadow, shadowy eye sockets, a shadowy, dangerous mouth.

Voices outside, someone rattling the door, the engaged bolt pressing against the loosely attached metal loop. When I step outside again, no one's there. An empty Twinkies bag in the bushes.

—

Samson Occom, AN ACCOUNT OF THE MONTAUK INDIANS, ON LONG ISLAND (1761):

The priests of Montauk said they obtained their arts from dreams, from nocturnal visions, from the devil, who appears to them in various forms, sometimes in the shape of this or that creature, sometimes as a voice etc.

—

F., waiting with a Dunkin' Donuts cup in hand at the gas pumps, illuminated by the floodlights. Eighty miles to Montauk, he calculates.

He talks about the ruins of the Palais Sans Soucis as he saw them one summer a few years ago when he went there from Cap-Haïtien: the view from the stairs of the palace to the green wooded hills.

The Honda is the last vehicle still on the road. Gusts of wind drive across the unlit road from the open water, the bushes at the side of the road in constant, incalculable motion. Now and then a light signals the presence of people.

—

I wake up after midnight. I am in a dark room, with only a little light coming through the diamond-shaped window in the door. I recognize a plasma TV at the foot of the bed, and on the wall above me a fanned thread of artificial flowers reminds me of the wreaths and arrangements placed on the coffins of the dead in funeral parlors. I listen to the roar of the surf, the regular, moderate rolling of the waves. Next to me lies Max Frisch, asleep.

—

Philip Roth brings Max Frisch in his New York hotel his book *MY LIFE AS A MAN*. Frisch's scruples about German "life as a man," although that is just what he wants to examine in *Montauk*.

To turn everything on its head as a test—I say on the phone when A. answers—while obvious, is also always enlightening.

As when, for example, I was at the Basel Opera with Laura recently and saw before it began that a woman was standing at the podium before the orchestra, I almost burst into tears.

It was as if she were an envoy, a first herald of the coming liberation, who spoke to us from her pedestal, telling us about the future with her baton.

She was so funny and conducted so nonchalantly.

—

After Frisch:

Then he went back to the car again. She waits; they have time. A whole weekend. [...] She usually doesn't like to wait. It occurred to him that he does not actually need his bag in order to see the Atlantic. (p. 7)

One time, a swampy ditch where she had to help him, and since then he leads the way. (p. 8)

She has vouched that she can find the car again, and he seems to trust her. Then, in order to light the pipe, she has to stop for a moment; it's windy, five matches are necessary, and in the meantime he has gone on ahead, so that for moments at a time she can no longer see him; some moments it seems to her like a fantasy or like a distant memory: this walk with a young man. (p. 8)

—

Indeed: F.'s fear of *poison ivy* as we walk through the bushes down to the sea. He takes small, careful steps. Then, fearful of slipping on the uneven stones below the lighthouse and falling into the sea, he stays behind.

When I return, he's sitting on a rock waiting, typing away on his iPhone.

—

MY LIFE AS PHILIP ROTH

—

The water backs up on the roads to form black, seemingly bottomless lakes. The last restaurant still open is a hot dog place on Montauk Point State Parkway. We eat under the glaring ceiling light with our reflections in the floor-to-ceiling windows, against which the rain beats.

She views him with pleasure when he dines. (p. 105)

The people behind the counter, even the waitress in the café, all speak Haitian Kreyòl here, he notes.

That does not happen in Frisch.
   No.

Nor the merchant ship that landed nearby in 1839, after the men and children abducted from the Sierra Leone area and destined to work on the Cuban sugar planta-tions had tried revolting on board and freed themselves.

—

The receptionist is asleep in front of her computer, while on TV the presidential candidate wanders across the stage of the TV studio.

—

The priests of Montauk, according to Occom, are ex-perienced in dealing with poison and poisoning. Some poisoned persons, he wrote, reported great pain; oth-ers just felt stranger and stranger until they went com-pletely out of their minds: "Sometimes they ran into the water; sometimes into the fire; and at times they ran up to the tops of tall trees and fell headlong to the ground, but were always unhurt."

He does not understand—writes Occom, himself a member of the Mohegan, a teacher, and a Christian missionary—he does not understand why this is not considered just as true as witchcraft in England or other nations, but instead treated as a great mystery of dark-ness etc.

—

Again I wake up after midnight but this time I know im-mediately that I am in the Albatross Motel in Montauk: the clammy sheets, the dampness in all the rooms.

There's a book on my chest and the bedside lamp is on: I must have fallen asleep reading. I bend to the side to turn off the light, and at that moment I see a shadow moving rapidly along the wall. I freeze, my hand on the lamp switch. Cautiously, I turn my head and look over my shoulder, but the room seems empty and unchanged behind me. F. has put a hand on his chest in his sleep; his breathing is slow.

Not much time can have passed when I wake up again to the sound of the room door swinging open and closed lightly. Outside, in the light of the fixture mounted on the exterior wall, is a white pickup truck that drove up in the early evening. Sand strewn on the red planks in front of the door. Besides the sound of the surf, nothing can be heard. I breathe shallowly, searching the room with my eyes without moving so as not to reveal that I'm awake and, I think in this moment, still alive.

Suddenly it seems essential to me to close the door. I get out of bed and step across the room, feeling strangely composed. From the outer pocket of my suitcase I pull the simple folding knife with which I quartered a pear on the drive through the Hamptons.

Instead of closing the door, I step out of the room into the open air. The night is cool, which, like for a fever patient, is quite pleasant to me. As if I know what I'm looking for, I walk toward the coast; I leave the parking lot and make my way through the waist-high bushes that shield the motel from the beach. Without feeling the pain, I feel the branches scratch my legs, and I hear my breath, my own gasping. Every now and then I look over my shoulder, and I always think I can just see my pursuer, who will catch up with me in a moment, but in reality I only ever see the same empty scenery.

Then I'm standing at the open sea, the beach sloping steeply in front of me. The foam-capped waves rolling toward me leave black marks on the sand. The deafening roar of the Atlantic and the incessant movement of the water make me lose sight of the situation: I know that any moment now, someone could pounce from any side without me being prepared.

Determined to throw myself at any danger, I clutch the handle of the knife, and I imagine myself lunging at something that could be a man or an animal, a moving, elusive mass, and stabbing again and again, uninhibited and frenzied, and when I finally stand, the bloody knife in my hand, I can see my dilated pupils, the mad whites of my eyes, my distorted mouth, and I move across the island, carrying my knife in front of me, an heirloom that over many generations has been passed down to me; I leave a trail of destruction, and my only disadvantage is that I am so white that you can see me from afar in the moonlight.

—

The trail along the teepees is thick with the footprints of the palefaces.

(Olivia Ward Bush-Banks, *Indian Trails: or Trail of the Montauk*)

—

Frisch, walking across the island: as he goes, he bends back the branches that reach into the path, touches the trunks of the pitch pines as if taking them into his inventory, touches the huckleberry, the gale bush, prairie grass rustling under his feet.

The writer makes the island arable.

I myself don't know how it could be done any better: not to take the things I describe, not to want them, and not to diminish them or determine them so clearly, but on the contrary to make them even freer and more independent than they were before I first set my eyes on them.

—

When I saw him, C., for the first time: far away on an escalator or walking on the edge of golden fields.

I didn't lift a finger, just looked. And how beautiful it was, this devotion, this study.

—

The uncanniness of the island—I say to A.—seems to have to do with the fact that the real place and the one I read about in Frisch's work, the one I thought I knew, were now to a certain extent lying on top of each other, and ghostly superimpositions and deviations thereby came to light.

Above all: the couple's eerie misconception that they are alone here. I see them, the European and the younger, red-haired American following a path through the undergrowth—far behind them the parking lot where they have left their blue Ford, a rental car. Deserted area.

Page 52:

"At one point, a Coca-Cola can in the grass, so they can't be the first people here."

—

In the case of PHARAOH v. BENSON et al. (1910) on the claim of Montauk Point land:

"There is now no tribe of Montauk Indians. It has been disintegrated and absorbed into the mass of citizens. If I may use the expression, the tribe has been dying for many years."

—

As if the past only just protruded into the couple's private present in the form of a Coke can: the can as a sign in the grass, a reference thrown into the text of a second, parallel island, densely populated and connected with world events in any number of ways.

That island where the Kreyòl-speaking snack-bar employees collect money in a jar next to the cash register to send relief supplies to Haiti.

On which the televisions transmit the images of the presidential debate.

On which the Montauk hunt wild birds and count among their gods those of the four corners of the earth: the god of the East, the god of the West, the god of the North, the god of the South.

Off the coast of which sits a black schooner (*La Amistad*) with torn sails, food scattered on deck, broken boxes, tattered fabric.

—

Summer 1839: *The Amistad* would have taken the men and children bought in the Havana market to the Cuban port of Guanaja farther east and from there to the plantations of Puerto Príncipe, but the men had armed themselves with knives made from sugarcanes on the way, killed the captain and the cook, and demanded that their owners take them back across the Atlantic to the West African coast.

Instead, the Spaniards sailed on a zigzag course northward: After two months, the far tip of Long Island ("The End"/Montauk Point).

—

The couple hiking across the island: they have left the blue Ford in the empty parking lot. They think they are alone.

(First shot of a horror movie.)

Then the crushed red can as a sign of human life, as a disturbing trace. The nervous glance over one's own shoulder: Is someone there?

Paranoia.

Where the real spooks—says F., as he puts on his socks—are the white couple that walks obliviously across the island.

—

Occom in his report "THE MOST REMARKABLE AND STRANGE STATE SITUATION AND APPEARANCE OF INDIAN TRIBES IN THIS GREAT CONTINENT" of 1783:

"...and when I Come to Consider and See the Conduct of the Most Learned, Polite, and Rich Nations of the World, I find them to be the Most Tyranacal, Cruel, and inhuman oppressors of their Fellow Creatures in the World, these make all the confusions and distructions among the Nations of the Whole World..."

Ávila

Addendum about Wakefield's carriage:

In England, young women of good family, writes Flora Tristan in the *Promenades dans Londres,* are forced to lead such dull, boring lives, so they turn to novels and begin to fantasize under the influence of those books: "[T]hey dream only of abductions." More specifically, says Tristan, of an abduction that "takes place in a magnificent four-horse carriage."

Mostly they waited in vain and then married, late, to a simple clerk, etc.

—

I found today a little booklet about Teresa of Ávila, the Seraphic Virgin,
    Princess of Spanish Mysticism,
    a "flaming figure," according to the hagiographer, who wanders through the "burning landscape" on the western edge of Europe, through that "land of strange fantasy,"
    not far, in actuality, from Africa.

—

I filed in a folder last year an image of the *Ecstasy of St. Teresa:* The rapt expression on her face, her slightly open mouth suggesting a moan, the ecstatic woman's head craned back, was carved by Bernini in white Carrara marble in Rome in the seventeenth century.

—

A note from her father, Alonso Sánchez de Cepeda: "On Wednesday, the twenty-eighth of March in the year fifteen hundred fifteen (1515) at five o'clock in the morning, more or less (for it was almost daybreak that Wednesday), my daughter Teresa was born."

TERESA DE AHUMADA

Her mother, Beatriz Dávila y Ahumada, married her husband, a *judeoconverso,* very young, and at sixteen gave birth to a first child who, like all subsequent siblings, bore the mother's name or that of the paternal grandmother so as not to betray any hint of the father's Jewish ancestry.

Her father, Teresa writes in her *Libro de la vida*, was virtuous and read good books; he also could never have brought himself to own slaves, like his brother, for example.

According to Victor García de la Concha, Theresa's mother had a "secret library."

—

I wake up after midnight, descend the stairs, and lo and behold: the door to my mother's secret library is open. A complete waste of time, memorizing the password ("Derevaun Seraun").

—

Teresa de Ahumada on her mother: "She was fond of chivalric novels," maybe because they distracted this woman who was always giving birth from her pain. She, Teresa, also read these books day and night (they suited her romantic nature, writes the hagiographer). Mother and daughter would quickly finish their work so that they could return to the books; this displeased the father.

During this time, she begins to wear gold, associates with a foolish cousin, passes the time with the house-maids, loves "shimmering gems, sumptuous fabrics, beautifully carved reliquaries," and even a man. She indulges in all sorts of frivolities.

When she walked through Ávila, the hagiographer says, people stared after her, as beautiful and sensual as she was.

At that time, she was threatened by her "tendencies pulling into the void." And even much later, after she had already passed through the monastery gate, she only ever sat in the consulting room and chatted, though in the monastery.

She is given to the Augustinian nuns of the convent of Nuestra Señora de Gracia, "where," she writes, "girls of my kind were educated."

—

Earlier, Teresa de Ahumada as a child next to a dovecote in Gotarrendura.

With her brother Rodrigo de Cepeda in their parents' house in town: together they read the legends of the saints. Teresa de Ahumada is six years old. She also urgently wants, like the women of the legends, to die a martyr. Not because of her love for God, but because she wants to enjoy the things, the *great goods* that exist in heaven, as soon as possible.

The seven- or eight-year-old Rodrigo de Cepeda and his younger sister Teresa de Ahumada deliberate over the open books of the saints.

In front of the parish church of San Juan Bautista stands Beatriz, the mother, a child in her arms, the fourth she has given birth to in the last four years.

The father, Alonso Sánchez de Cepeda, pages through the Lunarium.

Leafs through the poems of Virgil.

Through the *Retablo de la Vida de Cristo*.

Teresa de Ahumada and Rodrigo de Cepeda decide to travel to the *Land of the Moors* to ask that their heads be cut off. With food in their pockets, the children leave the townhouse in Ávila to go and lay down their lives in the name of Christ. They travel out of the city through the Puerta del Adaja and over the bridge, but not without stopping briefly at Nuestra Señora de la Caridad in the Lazarus hermitage. Only when they are already on the road to Salamanca are they discovered by an uncle, who returns them home.

The whole thing was Teresa's idea, says Rodrigo de Cepeda.

They read and understand that suffering and glory outlast this transitory world, and therefore they often say to each other: *forever, forever!* As if it were a secret slogan, whereby they might recognize each other in an as-yet distant future.

Since the plan to die a martyr's death was doomed to failure, in the garden of the estate in Gotarrendura, they build hermitages to live a secluded, pious life, but the small stone buildings keep collapsing.

Teresa de Ahumada as a child who, in concert with the other girls, constructs entire convents.

Beatriz Dávila y Ahumada, who wrote her will in the last days of 1528.

They carried her body out of the house in Gotarrendura.

Crosses and other signs of piety carved into the walls of the dovecote.

—

If it was said of Ellen West—I say to A.—that she bites greedily and lustfully into all life, the same can be claimed of Teresa de Ahumada:

A six-year-old fanatic who wants to surpass everyone and ascend straight to heaven,

long years torn between the world (*mundo*)—the chatter in the monastery's consulting room, the shimmering gems—and the truth (*verdad*),

later, ecstasy (*ékstasis*: stepping out of oneself, being outside oneself).

How EW wants to live among the poor as a Russian nihilist and promote the *great cause*.

How she always stands hungry before the cupboard where the bread is, which she just can't leave alone.

—

I'm standing in front of the cupboard where the bread is:

J'ai faim.

Once a few years ago, I was hurriedly walking along Hohlstraße toward Kalkbreite, sandwich in hand, and one of two painters in painter's pants on the bench by the streetcar stop called to me: Don't eat so greedily.

The pedestrian on a street corner near Kew Gardens: Come on, lady, smile.

After I get drunk, always the fear that I talked too much, that I had let myself go.

In contrast, the father who says to the mother: She didn't open her mouth again.

Did not part the lips.

Grimaced (twisted the mouth).

—

"Blessed are You, Lord, for putting up with me for so long! Amen."
   (*The Book of My Life*, p. 96)

—

– You're Catholic, right?
– That's how I'm registered in any case, and I also pay the church tax.
– Did you actually go to church?
– As a child, yes. On Tuesdays, our parents sent us to the school mass. That meant that each time we were all given fifty centimes with which we could buy a Bürli on our way to school after Mass. In case you don't know it, that's a small, very good bread with a dark, flour-dusted crust.
– The Mass was in the morning?

– At seven or half past seven – in any case, early enough that we could still get to school on time afterward. I was always thinking of the bread that we would buy at Brander – that's the baker's name. Imagine a round roll with a relatively hard crust, which you then break open, and the inside is very white and soft and dense. In some ways, the thought of this bread completely took over every Tuesday. You might say it all happened in His name, and I was not the only one for whom this was true: everyone ran to Brander's right after and bought a Bürli. Of course, we used to sit in the pews and listen to how the Lord took bread and broke it and said, "Take and eat of it, all of you: this is my body which is given for you." And then we would go up and have the host placed in our hands.

– Did you like doing that?

– The communion?

– Going to Mass in general.

– I think I was a pretty docile child, in the sense that I did many things without thinking anything, that is, without understanding or rejecting them either: I just sat there and waited. When I say that now, I think: an idiotic child. I know, for example, that I stared at one of the two inner side altars for hours…really for years: It depicts – I researched it just recently – St. Sebastian, who was tied to a tree trunk and then shot by Numidian archers. And he has a very nice body, very pale, his Roman toga slipped or torn away to his waist while they were dragging him to this tree. And in the left thigh, and in the chest near the heart, are the arrows of the Numids. But I don't remember having once had an insightful or exploratory thought about this depiction in all the years

I looked at the altar: I just stared.

– So there was no phase of religious fervor for you as a child either, as some people are known to have?

– No, although I was always moved by the ritual, the solemn proceedings, and by something I experienced as a dark devotion.

– What do you mean by that—dark devotion?

– Something ritualized, unconscious. In a chapel very close to my parents' house, every evening in May—the month of Mary—the women from the nearby houses came together for devotion. Peasant women, mothers, old women, they knelt in the narrow benches and prayed the rosary, a monotonous chant that passed effortlessly over their lips, and they must have lost themselves in prayer, perhaps finding themselves walking again over newly mown meadows or somewhere else completely different; in any case, far away, and in my memory it's dark in the chapel, only the one candle that they lit at the beginning is burning, and the women wear black costumes, the habits of Spanish nuns, but that's not true of course.

—

Teresa de Ahumada feels "great distaste for convent life," but when she sees a sister who begins to cry while praying, for example, she becomes jealous.

—

She doesn't want to become a nun—I say to A.—but she's also afraid of marriage: the choice between a

157

religious order and marriage in the end is the decision to give birth (like her mother) or not to.

And if the good life is understood to be one that is lived with a certain intensity, that is savored completely, why not a radical, extreme devotion, the discovery of emptiness, the ecstasy?

I understand that well.

Ecstasy as removal from a place, as a getting-outside-oneself.

The dictionary renders the Greek *ekstatikós* as both *maddening* and *mad*—I say to A.—or, as Eveline's mother said: "I have been there; you should go there" / "The end of the song is raving madness."

In any case, on November 2, 1535, Teresa de Ahumada enters the convent of La Encarnación in Ávila. When she leaves the townhouse and her father early in the morning, she feels as if every one of her bones is loosening inside her.

—

Enthusiasm of the novice about the life in the monastery; desire to die of a disease in order to quickly reach the eternal goods. (Ellen West kissing children with scarlet fever.) An exercise in turning away from the world; she feels sorry for those who still chase after it (*mundo*).

Great internal unrest.

Fainting spells like the ones she has known before; something seems to be wrong with her heart.

—

Then Teresa de Ahumada, at the end of 1538, on the way through the wintry province to Castellanos de la Cañada: Her father has sent her to Becedas for a cure from a healer known far and wide, a "curandera."

On the way, her uncle Pedro de Cepeda gives her the *Third ABC* in Hortigosa. At her sister María de Cepeda's, the sick woman waits out spring. In April she reaches Becedas.

The priest of Becedas, Pedro Hernández, who hears Teresa de Ahumada's confession, wears a copper amulet around his neck. It signifies a bond between him and an unfortunate woman with whom he has had relations for almost seven years. Teresa de Ahumada tells him to throw it into the river.

And if they had not had God alone on their minds, she and the pastor, between them there could have been a serious transgression too.

—

In the evening, Ortega y Gasset's *On Love* (1933) in hand.

CONTENTS

Page 145: The "strange lexical interchange between love and mysticism" as an indication of the deep kinship between the two.

The lover, as well as the mystic, turns toward one of these (the course of a brook, the beloved, His Majesty Jesus Christ) and in this way, away from everything else at the same time: "A great letting go of all things."

Page 157: "The urge to go out of oneself has produced all forms of orgiasm: drunkenness, mysticism, infatuation, etc."

—

Seen from the train window at Uzwil station, chalk crosses on the asphalt. **J3SUS, I am always with you!**

—

The cure in Becedas almost kills Teresa de Ahumada; bystanders must have already thought she was dead, because she later finds the wax on her eyelids they used at that time to seal the eyes of the dead.

—

In the consulting room of the Incarnation Monastery, Teresa de Ahumada sees with the eyes of her soul Christ's face in great rigor (1538?).

1556 or 1557: "such a sudden rapture that it almost tore me out of myself." The Lord wants her from then on to converse only with angels.

On the feast of St. Peter and Paul in 1560, she thinks she feels Christ beside her. She cries with fear, but as soon as he speaks to her, she calms, is again "filled with delight and without any fear."

A few days later he shows her his hands, which are of very great beauty; shortly after, his face.

Likely on January 25, 1561, she sees the Risen Lord. Compared to the light that accompanies these visions, the sun seems quite lightless.

Now and then a vision of the Lord on the cross, in the garden, or with a crown of thorns.

Several times an angel to her left, who seems to be on fire. He thrusts a long, golden arrow into her heart and pulls it out again. She burns with love for His Majesty: the great pain triggers an overwhelming tenderness.

"14. On the days that this lasted, I was in a daze. I would have preferred to see and speak nothing, but only to give myself over to my pain, which meant greater glory for me than all that exist together in the created world."

—

Don't you want—I write to C.—don't you want to see the church that I built in the last weeks and months with my own hands, its dome is bigger than that of the Milan Cathedral; that is, don't you want to say Mass with me finally? I've been ready for Holy Communion with you for a long time.

—

Mystical enthusiasm, writes Ortega y Gasset, is also known to the poet, who constantly thinks of his invented persons, e.g.,

"Balzac, when he breaks off a business conversation with the words, 'Eh bien, let us return to reality. Let's talk about César Birotteau!'"

Likewise lovers, in whose eyes their beloveds have, in a distinct sense, hijacked the world.

And is it not possible to say something similar of the explorers and conquerors, in whose feverish waking dreams only the *New World* figures? Hallucinations of sugar mountains, rivers of gold, untouched lands: "The urge to get out of oneself" manifesting itself in European fleets.

—

Eveline, who, when she must decide for or against the crossing on the night ship, thinks of her mother's words: *Derevaun Seraun!* ("The end of the song is raving madness.")

—

In any case, it is said that Teresa de Ahumada's brothers all emigrated "to the newly discovered lands of the West Indies (Las Indias)," where no one was interested in their Jewish ancestry.

Hernando de Ahumada leaves Spain around the year 1530,

Rodrigo de Cepeda follows the conquistador Juan de Ayolas on an expedition along the Paraná and Paraguay rivers and supposedly dies "in the wilderness of the Gran Chaco on the Río de la Plata fighting the natives."

Lorenzo and Jerónimo de Cepeda travel to Panama in the wake of the Spanish judge Cristóbal Vaca de Castro, and from there possibly via Buenaventura, Cali, and Popayán to Quito,

Antonio de Ahumada and Pedro de Cepeda leave Europe on one of the fifty ships of the fleet of the first Viceroy of Peru, who is the brother of Teresa de Ahumada's godfather Francisco Velásquez Núñez Vela,

Hernando de Ahumada carries a flag into the Battle of Iñaquito in January 1546,

during the battle, Antonio de Ahumada suffers head injuries that he will not survive,

Pedro de Cepeda explores Florida in Ponce de León's wake, allegedly later becoming a melancholic,

Agustín de Ahumada is the last of the brothers to cross the Atlantic in 1544 or 1546, fights in Chile against the Mapuche, becomes governor of Tucumán and father of a girl (Leonor),

Lorenzo de Cepeda marries the daughter of a conquistador in Lima; she bears seven children and dies before she's thirty.

Meanwhile, the ecstatic sister at home lets all things go.

Reno

– How are you?
– Good.

—

Yesterday, I biked up to the Max Frisch Archive. The head of the archive says, as we stand in front of his computer and he clicks through the digital copies, that it is not possible to quote from the typescripts directly,
nor from the questions Elisabeth Johnson noted for Frisch after reading the *Montauk* manuscript, including one about the passage on Roth / MY LIFE AS A MAN.

Instead, he pulls out a few books for me about Frisch and the American continent (*America!, Five Places in the Life of Max Frisch, Swiss Discover America,* etc.).

Somewhere in Frisch's records from Reno, Nevada, where he spent a night in the casino:
"Spooky impression, everywhere people are standing in front of the luck machines, throwing money in and manipulating. [...] The losers save face, but tremble in their fingers.

—

The memory of F. during a car ride telling me about a casino on the outskirts of Philadelphia, *The Sugarhouse*.

Watering plants at night, although C. recently advised against it.
But I am listening,
how greedily they drink:
glug, glug, glug.

—

Message to the reporter (Müller) who portrayed the lotto king Bruni for Swiss TV in the '80s: I would very much like to see, if possible, your films etc., kind regards.

Only later, the thought that the existence of the films means that he, Müller, must himself have been present at the auction on Lake Thun and must have seen close up what I know only as moving images on TV: the women and men bending over the property of the ruined gambler in the Bären restaurant in Spiez:
a cream-colored set of upholstered furniture, wine racks, a Karabiner 31 rifle, the two figures of dark wood or polished stone.

—

To the drunkard, the mystic, and the lover, whom Ortega y Gasset lists in INFATUATION, ECSTASY, AND HYPNOSIS as tending toward the orgiastic—I say to A.—should be added not only the immoderate eater but also the *gambler* who spends his feverish nights in front of the machines in the *Sugarhouse* that flash so promisingly.

However, it is the lottery player who seems to be a strange exception to this principle; having set up his game in an almost Protestant manner so that the only brief moment of excitement occurs on Saturday evening when, during the drawing of the lottery numbers on television, the numbered white balls roll back and forth in the drum for a while, crash into each other, pile up, and then singly find their way into the cylinders.

—

It has suddenly become warm again, first thing in the morning the windows are opened, there are so many birds outside here, and because the neighbors spread seed on their balconies, I keep seeing titmice and sparrows rushing toward the building out of the corner of my eye—pure madness at six o'clock in the morning, as if I lived in a large aviary.

—

Read Gerhard Meier, *Plants and Clouds*, buy myself all his books on the internet just for his cloud descriptions: the clouds of the nights, clear clouds, clouds over the Jura "like an unrolling abstract painting of enormous length."

—

On May 17, 1979, Bruni is a guest on the program *Music & Guests*. On April 28, not three weeks earlier, the drawing of the lottery numbers had made him king.

Now he sits there at a small table in a light blue suit, a tone almost identical to the blue tablecloth. Behind the newly crowned king is his wife and his boss; before him is a glass of orange juice. Flowers.

The Pepe Lienhard Band open the show with the piece "Café, Café": Lienhard and the horn players in colorful, shiny suits, red spotlight, and then a dancer: a black woman with a flower behind her ear and a white flower or shell wreath around her neck. So somehow Pacific or perhaps related to the Caribbean, the Brazilian coffee plantations after all, I don't know, and then a second dancer enters the frame, she too is black, her red dress cut low, almost to the navel.

Pepe Lienhard plays the flute. The musicians sing "café, café, café."

And there—the pictures prove it—sits WB, the reticent king, among the guests in the studio, watching.

—

Later I also found the Spiez auction in the TV archive. The recording starts a few seconds earlier than in the version I already know. For sale are some bottles of wine. Then the two figures: *So ladies and gentlemen we move onto the exotic as you see here*

—

How reluctantly I write this into the text, the description of the dancers: Because in language a future wants to be imagined and attempted in which this way of looking and the words belonging to it have long been completely irrelevant,

and when we get that far, in this future, this text will be also completely of yesterday.

Like when I stumble upon such linguistic relics in the texts of past decades and centuries that immediately strip them, the texts, of everything visionary and transform them into pure documents of their time.

Or, as Michel-Rolph Trouillot writes at one point:

"One will not castigate long-dead writers for using the words of their time [...] I am not suggesting that eighteenth-century men and women *should* have thought about the fundamental equality of humankind in the same way some of us do today. On the contrary, I am arguing that they *could not* have done so."

Just as the Haitian Revolution was unthinkable for the most radical thinkers of the European Enlightenment.

—

I wake after midnight and go downstairs. In the living room, the lotto king is dancing to the music of the Pepe Lienhard Band that blares from the TV set's speakers. The light from the screen falls flickering into the room. The dancing king has his arms stretched out to either side and is swaying his head back and forth in time to the music; he turns on his axis with flailing arms, moving his lips to the lyrics: *café*, *café*, *café*.

I knock loudly against the wooden door frame, and when the dancing man notices me, he turns one last time and then, swaying lightly, stands still. Listen, I'd like to sleep, I say, it's already late and I'm tired, but unfortunately at this volume, it's not possible. Immediately, the great king bends over the television and turns it off. Then he sits down on the sofa, hunched, his head propped up in his hands. I'm sorry, I say. Yes, all right, he waves it off, all right, no problem at all.

—

– How are you?

– I'm in over my head.

– The underbrush you were talking about?

– Fine by me, if that's what you want to call it.

– Can you say more about it?

– Everything becomes too much for me. At the beginning, I thought I had to somehow gather everything together, bring it all together, but now things are imposing themselves on me virtually—I see signs and connections everywhere, as if I had found a theory of everything, which is of course utter nonsense.

– But I imagine that is generally pleasing, the realization that, as I understand you now, all of a sudden sense can be made.

– There is an episode from my childhood that is fondly recounted in my family: how my father as a forester once drove up to an alpine pasture, taking me with him for a reason I don't know. I must have been five or six years old; in any case, I remember looking out of the windows of the white Jeep at the mainly treeless regions, rocky slopes against the dull sky. After the drive up to the alp via the steeply inclined road, we were standing at the edge of a mountain lake as my father talked to the farmer who was summering his animals there; I, the child, saw a goat some distance away. And you know how it is: its white fur shone at me, so naturally I wanted to get close to the goat. I wanted to solve the riddle that the goat, standing like a phantom in the middle of the meadow, posed to me, but even then I knew of course that it wouldn't be so easy to get close to her under the circumstances: I had to commend myself to the animal, I had to find a language with the goat, I had to make it understand that I wanted to look at it but not kill it. Every child knows about the unpredictability, the stubbornness of animals. They often escape at the last moment. What I want to say: As I was facing this goat, which was not much smaller than I was, as we were facing each other eye to eye, I started here, with this foregoing considerations. I fully expected that my attempts would remain fruitless.

– But?

– But no sooner had I, the child, made the plan to commend myself to the goat, than behind this animal other goats entered the meadow, and together they instantly came rapidly toward me, the farmer's whole herd trotting in my direction. You can imagine that I was cheered at the prospect of the goats coming so voluntarily, and my father might have said something like "Look, the goats are coming." The farmer, on the other hand, would not have been interested in his animals, heading so purposefully toward me, a child who was hardly taller than these goats. They surrounded me, pushed their way near me; the ones in the back stood on their hind legs so that they could see me over the heads of the ones in front. I remember their cool, watery eyes, funny eyes; their narrow heads and the bright noses with which they nudged me; and then their tongues, which they began to run over my hands and face.

I see exactly how the child tries to drive away these spirits, which she wanted to call to her only moments ago—now with both hands; how over and over she pushes the meddlesome animals away, which then pounce on her again so unrestrainedly, which besiege her. The father and the farmer are amused: the goats have never harmed anyone before. But it is too much for the child: she sees only the tongues and the open mouths, she feels the bodies of the goats on her own body and the hooves with which they trample her feet, and she begins to cry loudly. Much later, in the back seat of the car, she is still exhausted and stunned.

– Is that how you see yourself now?

– Except that in this case the goats are now disembodied.

– But it's true that the goats, as your father and the farmer said, are actually quite harmless.

– But the desire to speak with the goat, to understand the goat, that is, under the circumstances, not without its dangers.

—

– I've thought a bit longer about what you said regarding the goats. And what occurred to me: famous mediums after their sessions all experience a kind of breakdown and suffer from great exhaustion.

– A few days ago, after weeks of reading about St. Teresa's illnesses and ecstasies in the *Libro de la vida* and trying to make sense of them, my limbs suddenly began to ache a lot, or rather to tremble, so that I could hardly stand up for days. I dragged myself to the laundry room, and when I had to, I went for groceries, but that was all. My mother said on the phone that maybe I was iron deficient, many women suffer from that, so I took iron supplements and magnesium tablets and so on, you know. The point is that I realized very late how funny it was that just now, when I'm dealing with the fainting and the pains of the saints, I have this weakness that's actually without real cause. So I do believe that in these moments we move beyond what we understand and that it's quite exhausting. And I understand how, when too much is demanded of the medium, the conversation breaks off and the medium sinks as if they've been given an electric shock. The dictionary also says that the word that means "to suspect" or "to sense," *ahnen*, comes from the Middle High German *mir, mich anet*: "It comes to me," i.e., "I see ahead." The child is so tired because the goats have come so close to her.

Praia Bay

One of the first books I pick up after I've started to gather things in the square (NEW WORLD PLAZA), after I've started to look for analogies and sequels to that unsolvable scene in Spiez and to think about the *leap*, the leap across the gulf, is Flora Tristan's *My Journey to Peru*.

Tristan: daughter of Don Mariano Tristán y Moscoso and Anne-Pierre Laisnay. Leaves France in 1833 at the age of thirty aboard the *Mexicain* to seek out her Peruvian father's noble family in Arequipa and claim her inheritance. At that time, she is already a mother and has lived for months under a false name while fleeing from her husband.

He (Chazal) had indulged in gambling, sacrificing the profits of his business to the game.

I could have started with that. A first, inaccurate echo of the scene on the Thunersee, a transposition.

—

As we learned transpose in school: the mirroring and zooming in and out of geometric solids with unchanged aspect ratios.

—

Waking up without knowing who you actually are and what plans you went to bed with the night before. Rising from sleep through a long tunnel. The chirping of birds through the open window. Only gradually does it all come back to me, including C., like a distant memory, a landscape seen years ago in passing through the open car window, bleached out by the light.

—

– Recently, I woke after midnight. For a while I lay there without doing anything, then I got up, opened the door of the room I was in, and descended the darkened stairs: I was in my parents' house. From the bedrooms a wooden staircase that winds slightly at the lower end leads down to the ground floor, and I realized in that moment, because of that staircase, it was a dream, that I was therefore descending this staircase in a dream and was in truth still asleep. So, I go down this staircase, and already from the hallway I see that there is still a light on in the kitchen. With my arms stretched out to the sides, I feel my way forward to the bright shape of the open kitchen door, and then, even before the light catches and reveals me, I see my three aunts sitting in the kitchen. It smells of hashish and one of my aunts is pouring rum into little cups. And as I'm standing there in my nightgown, I immediately think of the first pages of *Heart of Darkness* and the men whose ship is lying off the Thames Estuary waiting for the tide to change — don't ask me why. Anyway, the aunts then see me and tell me to sit down with them, so I sit down and watch them smoke and play dominoes under the low-hanging lamp for a long time.

– Are they actually smokers, your aunts?

– No.

– That was the end of the dream?

– No. When I think it's getting light outside the kitchen window, one of my aunts asks me, without turning her face away from the game, how I'm doing, and I say, "Fine, fine"; as I see the leaves of the box tree slowly coming out of the darkness outside, I say, "I'm fine." The next moment I am sitting alone at the now clean and empty table. It's a winter morning, the thin branches of the rowan tree outside the window are covered with a fine layer of snow, and the sky is overcast but very bright. I get up and put a capsule in my parents' coffee maker. The sound of the machine is piercing. I then walk through the rooms of the house with the cup in my hand, all bathed in the same wintry light, and contemplate this system of rooms and chambers in which I spent my childhood and know as well as nearly anything else. On a shelf, small clay figurines that my father's brother — a former priest — brought from Peru when I was a child: an owl with wide eyes, a flute, a long-necked llama.

– Peru?

– Where he lived on behalf of a missionary society.

– So would you say it's something that continues into

your family, part of what you're trying to grasp here?
– Perhaps, yes. Although it must be said that mine is a very unremarkable family.
– Then you woke up in front of this shelf?
– Something like that.

—

In a program on Swiss television (*The King and his Boss*) the camera touches, at 49:36, one of the two figures that later come to Spiez on auction. There she stands on the shelf in the apartment of the worker and lottery king WB, intact, untouched,

in front of her is a small collection of inscribed stones and crystals, just like the one I took from the shelf in my grandfather's apartment after his death:

Rome Feb. 1980 Catacomb S. Callisto / Lourdes 1985 / Puna Desert Chivay 14.7.93 / Machu Picchu 21.7.1993 / Maras Salina Urub. 25.7.1993 / Ollantaytambo 26.7.93

—

The Limmat so green and languid today, hemmed in by green trees that hug the water's edge, their leafy branches reaching far out over the water as I pass them on the train, then the highway, the sky above rather childishly blue.

Because I've fallen behind on my notes, and because frankly, I'm fed up with writing everything down, I can't put all kinds of things in their proper places;

for example, that four days ago I was still standing on a platform at the Lyon-Part-Dieu train station, quite by chance. It was a Saturday morning, after which we drove on through the department of Ain to Geneva, where we drank orange juice and lattes and saw from afar the Jet d'Eau over the house roofs.

—

Or that I had been convalescing on the sofa for weeks: The pots and pans in which I had poached quail eggs and melted couverture—i.e., prepared the most select things—were piled up in the kitchen without the guest (C.) ever having arrived.

I cried on the phone: what a waste, etc.

—

The goats crowd my bedside at night, their white bodies shining bright in the moonlight that filters through the windows.

—

During her long crossing from France to Valparaíso, the *Mexicain* docks in Praia Bay because of a leak: The land of this Cape Verde island, writes Flora Tristan in the *Pérégrinations d'une paria*, is black and dry…banana bushes, mulberry fig trees, large-leafed plants, a church, the house of the American consul.

On the beach in Praia, Chabrié, the captain—whose cargo's value is slipping through his fingers because his ship is taking too long to get to Peru—hints at his love for Tristan, then cries.

Love—Tristan writes—was still a religion for her in the year of the crossing (1833) and since the age of fourteen: I thought of love as the breath of God. "Je considérais l'amour comme le *souffle de Dieu…*"

J'avais aimé deux fois, she writes, I've loved two times: once a young man who was too soft-hearted to assert himself with his father; and a second, coolly calculating—"un de ces êtres froids, calculateurs," to whom great passion appeared as madness.

The futility with which she loved both times did not diminish the greatness of her love, but after that she no longer expected to be understood by a man who was not capable of that great devotion commonly perceived as madness because it is entirely without self-interest,

that devotion of revolutionaries and martyrs.

—

With "mystical urge for redemption," it is said, she—whose life had been marked to the utmost by politics—promoted her idea of the **UNION UNIVERSELLE des Ouvriers et Ouvrières** in her last years.

"Engagement" in the dictionary as "commitment out of world-view or other attachment": the desire for a passionate, perhaps excessive attachment to the world, to bite greedily into all life.

—

In 1839, in a letter from London to a woman named Olympe: "You say you loved me and I magnetized you; indeed, even put you in ecstasy."

She herself feels a "burning thirst" to be loved: "But I am so demanding, so exacting, so gluttonous and gourmet at the same time that everything brought to me can scarcely satisfy my desire. My heart is like the Englishman's palate: it is a deep maw in which everything that enters it shatters, breaks, and disappears."

—

Immediately upon arrival in the bay of Praia, a small schooner from Sierra Leone (p. 27) is the first indication of the real significance of the Cape Verde island.

La traite: The inhabitants of Praia exchange slaves for flour, wine, oil, rice, sugar, and other things.

—

The sugarcane that the enraptured European crusaders first sucked in Jerusalem and in Acre is taken by the Europeans to the Atlantic islands and then across the Atlantic: to Madeira, to the Azores, to the Gulf of Guinea, to Brazil, etc.

In the Cape Verde Islands, too—where the first settlers still live off the animals left behind by the explorers—sugarcane is introduced to produce *aguardente* and sugar. But the land of these islands is too dry, so they switch instead to trading in people, and there develops in the fifteenth century the plantation society, as it would then be found in all areas of the tropical "New World" in the following centuries (Sidney M. Greenfield: *Plantations, Sugar Cane and Slavery*).

—

The slave trader of Praia: Even as a child, he tells Tristan, his parents had him destined for the priesthood; he attended the seminary of La Passe, near Bayonne, where he attracted attention for his religious zeal. When, in 1819, from all the seminaries of the country, the most zealous and most devoted were chosen for a mission to the savage peoples, the idolaters, the choice had fallen to him, and so he boarded a ship.

When he, Tappe, then learned en route that on this barren island—*sur cette terre de misère et d'aridité*—a quick fortune could be made from little money, he decided to stay.

During the meal aboard the *Mexicain*, still anchored in the bay, the seminarian eats so greedily that all his attention is on his glass and his plate. From his facial features, Tristan says, she could tell that his greatest passion is feasting (*la gourmandise*). With shining eyes and flared nostrils, sweat on his forehead, he contemplates the meat that is being served. He seems to be in

182

that state in which "the lust we cannot restrain streams out of all our pores."

He had married one of the women he owned and she would pre-taste everything he ate for him.

—

The young American consul, *representative of a republic*, beats a man covered in blood in the lower hall of his house.

The sweaty Tappe.

Tristan does not go into Praia for a week because of the smell of Africans, African children.

Visiting aboard the schooner from Sierra Leone: The Italian (Brandisco) serves rum, coffee, and cookies. Then he shows the guests a fifteen- or sixteen-year-old boy for sale.

—

On television, a film about the women of Cabo Verde, who today mine the fine black sand on the beaches of the archipelago to sell to developers.

Madame Adelaide: They are like the slaves of São Tomé and Príncipe who were in chains at that time.

—

In a passage—I say to A.—concerning Tristan's visit on board with the Italian captain, the word *cupidité*: the excessive desire (for money and riches).

The proximity of burning thirst, or the great and delicious wickedness called *grôze leckerheit* in the story of the half-pear, to the gluttony of the seminarian: is it merely the possibilities, opportunities, and the sheer power of the hungry that determine—I say—whether their desire can be formulated and satisfied, whether it manifests itself as destructive or, on the contrary, counteracts destruction—repairs something that was previously devastated, fills a crack with putty.

—

Paul Gauguin, Tristan's grandson ("II. Souvenirs de jeunesse"): She, Tristan, probably did not know how to cook—"Il est probable qu'elle ne sut pas faire la cuisine."

Gauguin's painting *The Artist's Mother* (c. 1893): on a bright yellow ground, a portrait of the young Aline Gauguin, Flora Tristan's daughter, as a strange mirror image of his earlier Tahiti painting *Vahine no te tiare* (*Woman with Flower*).

The former stockbroker Gauguin and his models in the French colony, his sculptures, his *Maison du Jouir* (*House of Pleasure*) on Hiva Oa Island, etc.

Plaisir 3

Summer 1802: A locked carriage leaves the port city of Brest late; it rolls along dark country roads through the department of Finistère, probably passing Montauban, Rennes, and Nantes, then Angers, Chapelle-Blanche. In Tours, where the horses are changed overnight, it is noted that one of the passengers is wearing three jackets despite the heat.

On 5 Fructidor (August 23), the carriage arrives in Pontarlier; with fresh horses it covers the last miles: on a steeply sloping hill in the French Jura, not far from the border with Switzerland is that castle, a fortress, which one of the two men in the carriage will not leave alive.

From Pontarlier, the sub-prefect writes: "Toussaint-Louverture arrived in Pontarlier today at half past one in the afternoon; he is accompanied by a servant."

—

In the report of his son, Isaac Louverture: two carriages and two companies of cavalry would have been waiting for his father and his *domestique* when they were taken offboard the *Héros*. Louverture had climbed into one, the servant into the other.

At night, they are forbidden from stopping in major cities.

When they passed Guingamp, there were some officers who served under Louverture in Saint-Domingue. They asked that the carriage stop so they could greet the prisoner being transported, their former general, the leader of the Haitian Revolution.

—

For a long time yesterday I sat in the nearly dark office and waited for the rain to end, but eventually had to go and was already completely soaked by the time I reached the stadium. The water ran in streams over my face and into my collar.

Then this morning, wisps of fog rising from the deep green flank of the Üetliberg. The whole city saturated with moisture.

Louverture, brought on a French navy ship (*Le Héros*) from Saint-Domingue to Europe, sees his wife, sons, and nieces, who were all transported with him, in Brest for the last time: he is followed into captivity in the Fort de Joux only by his servant Mars Plaisir,

un domestique
le dévoué serviteur
le fidèle Plaisir son domestique

When he enters the cell—according to Plaisir's report to one of Louverture's sons—he believes he is stepping underground.

—

On October 6, a message from the commander of Fort de Joux, Baille, to the prefect of the department: for twelve days Louverture has been asking for a cap because of constant headaches resulting from an injury from a firearm.

A NOTA is appended: He forgot to say that Toussaint Louverture adds sugar to everything he drinks. Since the prisoner used up his own sugar some time ago, he, Baille, had given him some of his. Now that he has again asked for sugar this morning, he seeks guidance in this matter.

—

By this time Mars Plaisir has already disappeared without further mention from Fort de Joux and from the literature: He had to leave the castle again on 20 Fructidor (September 7). Elsewhere: He was separated from Louverture after three months.

—

His further whereabouts a footnote (77) in Nemours' *Histoire de la captivité et de la mort de Toussaint-Louverture*: He was imprisoned in Nantes, then he

was able to return to Haiti and allegedly died there in
Port-au-Prince.

—

Baille, on October 9, 1802: Louverture had renewed his
request for sugar, and he, Baille, told him that the sugar
he had been giving him for the last fifteen days was his
own and that he would give him some more over the
next few days, but if the Citoyen Préfet did not give him
an order to provide sugar by then, he, Baille, could no
longer offer it at his own expense, since he was not at
all wealthy enough to do so.

Strictly speaking, Louverture asks for a sugarloaf (*il me
renouvelle la demande d'un pain de sucre*).

—

Préfet Jean de Bry to Citoyen Battandier: He had received two statements of expenditure from Citoyen
Baille pertaining to the prisoner Louverture and had
found irregularities,
     among other things, expenditures for sugar in the
amount of 12f. and 12f. 7c., totaling 24f. 7c.,
     which undoubtedly cannot be right, because—he
writes—consumption in this amount inside one month
would be *exorbitant*.

—

Geggus, p. 266:

The Haut-du-Cap plantation, where Toussaint Louverture was born, does not produce much more than 100,000 lbs of sugar even in a good year because of the region's thin and stony soil.

—

When I now return for the hundredth time to this place, this place where I gather everything, my gathering place, I see first the Haitian worker sleeping in the shade of a yew tree cut in the shape of a sugarloaf, then Adam Smith with the sugar bowl from his cousin's house—in general, islands & mountains of sugar; I see Mars Plaisir as a sculpture whose face is obscured by other things:

the Versailles-Chantiers train station,

Wakefield's carriage,

the *Harmony of the Seas* of the Royal Caribbean Cruise Line.

—

In August 1779, twelve years before the Haitian Revolution, Louverture, who was freed a couple of years prior, rents a coffee plantation from his son-in-law Philippe Jasmin Désir along with a man, four women and their eight children. One of them, the most expensive (Jean-Jacques), becomes known much later as Jean-Jacques Dessalines.

That General Dessalines, who in Kleist's *Betrothal* is just returning to Port-au-Prince with thousands of insurgents when one night the Swiss man knocks on the back door of Congo Hoango's house.

He must reach Port-au-Prince, says the Swiss, who is fighting on the side of the French, "before General Dessalines manages to encircle and besiege it with the troops he is leading."

Dessalines, who declared himself Emperor of Haiti (1804).

—

By the way—I tell A. on the phone—Kleist is arrested in January 1807 on his way from Königsberg to Berlin as a suspected spy: "The journey goes, as I have already told you," he writes to Ulrike von Kleist, "to Joux, a castle near Pontarlier, on the road from Neufchâtel to Paris."

Letter to Ulrike from April 23, 1807:
    They arrived at Fort de Joux on March 5.
"Nothing can be more desolate than the sight of this castle resting on bare rock. [...] We had to get out, climb, and ascend farther on foot; the weather was dreadful and the storm threatened to blow us down into the abyss from this narrow, ice-covered path."

Kleist's fellow prisoner, Gauvain, had been locked in the room "in which Toussaint Louverture had died."

—

Kleist, who writes in a letter on green postal paper to Wilhelmine von Zenge on October 10, 1801, that the Persian magi knew well the law that "a man can do nothing more pleasing to God than this, to cultivate a field, plant a tree, and beget a child," and thus decides to move to Switzerland to become a farmer.

In the spring of 1802, he moves into a house on the Aare Island in Thun, "quite enclosed by Alps, 1/4 mile from the city": an idyll with flowers and girls.

Meanwhile, the ship (*Le Héros*), with Toussaint Louverture on board, is reaching the open sea, taking the prisoner across the Atlantic to France.

—

Among the 635 Swiss sent from Ajaccio on the French warship *Le Redoutable* on February 4, 1803, to Port-au-Prince to fight alongside the French against the insurgents was a cousin of the landlord of the Thun Island house:

Maximilian Gatschet, twenty-one-year-old, died in *St Domingue* —

as did the greater part of the 1st Battalion of the 3rd Helvetic Half Brigade.

Purportedly, however, they had not gone voluntarily; they had tried to protest the "use of Swiss men overseas."

—

In a passage in Girard (*The Slaves Who Defeated Napoleon*): after Louverture's death on April 7, 1803, in his Fort de Joux cell, his few belongings were "auctioned off."

In light of this first auction—the auction of the things of a man who once counted among the property of a European, lived on the plantations, later sat on thrones adorned with silk and declared himself governor in the Constitution of 1801 *for the rest of his glorious life*, but in the end was forced to beg for sugar in a French prison—

in the light of this first auction (if it ever took place): the other, second auction again, the spectacle in Spiez, where the things of the plumber and one-time lotto king (WB) are sold off:

a karabiner rifle,

upholstered furniture,

two figurines said to be from Haiti.

As if they both, WB & Louverture, had stepped through a portal, an opening, and suddenly found themselves freed from the conditions that had determined them up to that point, only to realize a short time later that the *mistake* had been noticed immediately and was charged to them posthaste.

WB: *What was I punished for? I was never too big for my britches.*

—

If people will still follow me this far or read all this as a record of a madness, material for a case study…I say to A.: "Patient dreams that she is haunted by goats at night."

Spiez

Werner Bruni's memoirs are preceded by the *workers' motto*:

"Work on and work yourself blind. / Whoever can't finish the job will be left behind."

MY SKILLS NEVER END,
so to speak.

—

WB, born 1936, worker.

His father was a bricklayer's foreman, a marksman, a drunkard: backbreaking work had brought him into crisis.

The mother is employed in the dairy, takes in washing, and cleans houses to raise extra money but often cannot show herself in public after the husband comes home drunk and is violent because, for example, the food was not immediately ready.

Seven children.

—

Flora Tristan, **Le P O U R Q U O I je mentionne les Femmes** (*Union Ouvrière*, p. 57ff.):

When she was in Bordeaux in 1827, it happened that the husband of a grocer came home in the evening and the soup was not ready. They got into an argument about this, and when the man got physical and slapped her in the face, she, who had been cutting bread with a large kitchen knife, lunged at her husband in a rage, pierced his heart with the knife, and killed him.

The woman's grief over her husband's death had been immense, and since she had not committed her crime intentionally—moreover, since she had a four-month-old child to nurse—the investigating judge ruled to release her from prison. The grocer herself protested vehemently against her release: How could such a dangerous creature as she be released? the mother of seven cried. And when she was sent home anyway, she declared that she would see to justice herself and let herself starve.

Neither her own mother nor her children, neither the judges nor the priests nor the women from the market succeeded in dissuading her from her plan. So they tried another way: cakes and fruits, puddings, wine, and meat were brought to her room, and even poultry was roasted and served very hot so the smell would stimulate her appetite. But the greengrocer would not be persuaded: a woman who could kill a father of seven must die; she reportedly suffered great torment then died on the seventh day.

—

According to the book about the lottery king, WB — a laborer's son — was a delivery man for the butcher Däppen in the '40s, and later for a baker in the evenings and on Saturdays. There were "the fifteen-cent doughnuts, the small ones, and the thirty-cent doughnuts, the big ones. I thought he didn't count them. As far as I was concerned, they were countless."

He steals a sausage from the butcher, Däppen, and from the baker he ate one of his rolls because he was hungry. Got beaten, did not return.

Later, at the age of sixteen and off to Welschland: he should "learn to eat foreign bread." He works for a baker on Lake Neuchâtel, later in a bakery on Rue du Four in Yverdon. Sees to the wood for the ovens, delivers bread to the inns.

During this time, his father disappears; he is found five weeks later in the wintry Aare, identified by the engraving on his pocketknife.

—

– In my mother's accounts it was always that they, the sisters, had to deliver the meat, on a moped — if I remember correctly — and on the luggage rack was a basket full of sausages, even in winter. Or their father would drive up the steep roads with them in the car and then send them on foot through the snow over the last hundred meters with the basket.

—

Later: WB as an assistant for a plumber, as a recruit, in shirt and tie next to a Buick 1 convertible that doesn't belong to him. He goes out, frequents the dance halls for Sunday dances, gets laid off.

Then the entrepreneur Hauenstein hires him at his heating and plumbing company (February 1, 1960). WB carries oxygen cylinders up ten, twelve floors, cast-iron radiators, gas generators, pipes, distribution batteries; he welds connections, installs toilets and sinks in single-family homes, apartment blocks, the Holiday Inn, and the converted "Lake Rose" in Faulensee, etc.

—

"The way the Count slowly crushed his fine bread in his hand while speaking" (Ellen West), this careless gesture would almost certainly have been noticed by him, Bruni.

—

Hauenstein, the boss: also the child of a working-class family. Later he was a merchant, real estate dealer, multimillionaire.

Müller: "As a child, did you have the feeling that you could compensate for the love you lacked by earning money?"
– If you looked at his father, who was a brutally dominating person, then yes. The only times he had seen him laugh was when he had earned money and his father had gotten some of it.

In Müller's film *Der König und sein Chef* (*The King and his Boss*): Hauenstein's rise begins with a small "colonial goods" store that he runs in Steffisburg; he lays the foundation for his successful career with this store; it is this general store that helps him gain the necessary capital or represents his first capital that makes the difference between him and someone like WB.

—

In a later film of Müller's: two golden apples and a golden pear on a table in Hauenstein's house, located directly on the lake.

—

WB's stoic sincerity: despite the fact that, as he knows, the whole world is corrupt and only concerned with its own advantage, he, for his part, holds fast to his honesty as a worker.

He wants no more and no less pay than he is entitled to for the work he does. Does not want to receive anything as a gift. Doesn't want to owe anything to anyone. Wants to always do the best work.

As if he could be the example to heal the world, he willingly gives himself up and returns to the construction site over and over, even when a crane-load of steel pipes smashes his head in, even after working 48 hours straight and his heart giving up the ghost for a short time on the third day, even when he falls many meters into the depths while working in a tunnel.

—

At the intersection of Albisriederstraße and Aemtler-straße, I was almost run over by a red vintage car—look at that, a Buick 1 convertible, I think when I see the car coming my way but it's just some Citroën with the top down. We barely glide past each other and on through the warm summer evening.

—

And do you remember—I write to C.—how I once climbed up into the trees with the cone pickers at harvest time especially for you to get the precious pine nuts. I was sweating like crazy. How you then politely declined:
I would prefer not to.

Later I ate the seeds myself:
    they tasted exquisite;
    how small and soft they were.

—

In the evening, going through the city. Everywhere people are standing out in front of their houses, at three, four in the morning. They say it's a tropical night.

At some point I could only see the lights; oriented myself by the bright spots: the glowing ATM at the foot of Prime Tower, the empty office floors, orange streetlamps on the bridge.

Finally, I laid my forehead on the shoulder of an economist.

He loves Umberto Eco, he said.
    Works for a bank.

His mouth tasted sweet, sugar everywhere, sugary taste on his lips, tongue, his neat, beautiful teeth.

Because—he said—here: a candy in his mouth. Immediately the memory of the canister on the shoe cabinet in the hallway of my paternal grandparents' apartment, a glazed clay jar with a lid, in which they kept the candies that they guarded as if they were pieces of gold.

They didn't call them "candies"; they called them "sweets."

We circled the canister just like we circled the TV; when we visited, we couldn't leave it alone.

Said goodbye to Adam Smith at Hardbrücke station, walked home.

Lying on a bench in the park at seven o'clock, looking up into the increasingly bright sky with burning eyes (the eyes of the gambler or the nun).

—

A picture from *Illustrated Switzerland*: WB as a king with velvet cloak and heavy crown, his gaze directed upward, as if his eyes were following the trajectory of a flying body, as if receiving a prophetic message addressed to him alone.

—

Freud: Sweets and candies often represent *caresses* and *sexual gratification* in dreams. (From *The History of an Infantile Neurosis*, Chapter IX)

—

Judith is back from France, still very summery in her flowing dress, and puts *Madame Bovary* on the table: how Emma Bovary's maid night after night helps herself to a *heap of sugar* from the kitchen cupboard and eats it alone, in bed, after she has prayed.

Meanwhile, diagonally behind Judith is a woman bent over her coffee who is so thin, so gaunt, that everything alive seems to have gone from her face. The features of a dead woman. But she is quite beautifully and carefully dressed, as if it were the clothes that prevent her from leaving, from letting everything go.

—

Regardless, on the evening of April 28, 1979, the balls determine WB is the winner of 1,696,335.90 Swiss francs. He sits in front of the television and notes down the numbers. He has spent the afternoon playing cards at the Bären restaurant.

Later that evening, according to Bruni's memoirs, he, his wife and a third person took a walk around the reservoir in Spiez and had a drink at the Bären.

How the landscape must have appeared to them that evening: everything completely new, I imagine, suddenly new and light—the outlines of the mountains; the outlines of the trees in the twilight; the motionless, utterly dark surface of the reservoir.

And what they probably thought about: He (WB) had only ever wished to retire a little early, his body worn out from work. To take a few trips, to live in a small house with a garden.

Three days later, the new king, who has so far wisely kept his mouth shut, leaving only a message on his boss's answering machine, is summoned to Hauenstein's office (the office: on the top floor of the recently acquired "Rebell" ski factory). There he is awaited by photographers: it seems the boss had informed the press about WB's stroke of luck.

—

On May 3, 1979, the headline: "BLICK found the lottery millionaire—a laborer!"

The day before, the newspaper had contacted the seer Alfredo Gisler and the clairvoyant Claudhilde Näpflin from Buix to suss out the identity of the winner.

—

WB: "I was an ordinary worker and remained an ordinary worker. However, that I would have nothing left from the winnings—nothing at all, just my being a worker—that I never could have imagined."

How the 300 workers brought by Mr. Peel (according to Marx) to the Swan River in New Holland seek wide open spaces as they slip away to make themselves independent in this seemingly empty, promising land: a procession to be prevented because it meant that the common laborer would not remain a common laborer and that Mr. Peel's goods, tools, and machines would rot under a tent.

Similar to this exodus, the escape of those 300, is perhaps also the plumber's ascent: through an accidental gap in the fence he steps through into new circumstances.

—

An old *Spiegel* report ("Hier ist Totentanz") about "Lotto-Lothar" Kuzydlowski. The unemployed truck driver and carpet buyer from Hanover, who won 3.9 million marks in 1994, "escaped his fate as a loser," according to *Der Spiegel*, without making much effort, thinking, or even moving. Lotto Lothar "had done nothing at all. He had only been lucky."

Then, according to *Spiegel*, he buys a Lamborghini and goes on vacation eight times in 1996 alone and then once more, before Christmas, to Jamaica.

1995, an interview with *FOCUS*:

FOCUS: Have you ever thought about emigrating?

> *Lothar K.: No, why? I travel a lot, but other countries don't interest me that much. I'm just looking for sun and the beach. After two weeks we came back home. We want to stay here and live normally.*

FOCUS: But you became a millionaire overnight, that's not quite normal.

> *Andrea K.: I always say that anyone who is born rich and then ends up like us has a much harder time than if we ordinary people suddenly win something like that. We stay the way we were.*

—

The management of his profits, it can be read everywhere, is taken over by Hauenstein, the boss of the newly crowned man, who, according to WB, is a *super good* boss by the way and obviously knows something about dealing with money: he builds apartment blocks, high-rise buildings, thousands of apartments, invests in companies, owns a restaurant and hotel chain, and also drives a Ferrari.

He gets power of attorney over WB's account and sells him a so-called "twelve-plex," a twelve-family building in which he, the king, installed the pipes. Additionally, a duplex apartment: a millionaire could no longer live in the workers' neighborhood.

After deducting taxes, WB is left with three-quarters of a million in profit. For the twelve-plex, he takes out a mortgage of 1.25 million from the bank.

What else he buys: things for his wife, including two solariums. Photo equipment, a microwave, a Honda Accord.

—

When his downfall has been announced and the twelve-plex, which has grown increasingly empty, has already been sold again:
    The Caribbean Journey.

He highlights it himself—I say to A. on the phone—you could say it figures in his own narrative as the *happy time*.

—

Shortly before half past eight, the Air France plane de-parts the airport, rapidly gaining altitude and finally reaching the weatherless region of the atmosphere, and light is so sudden in the cabin that her seatmate, a man of perhaps 55, covers his eyes with a silent yelp. Every time this light—he says guiltily—this stable blue up here: he can't get used to it. As if—he continues, laughing softly—as if the most elementary knowledge about the system, the solar system in which they were living, had still not gotten through to him after so many centuries. A few hours ago, as he had watched how the airport employees directed the vehicles with their glow sticks on the tarmac of Milano-Malpensa in the rain, he had of course been able to imagine that, at the same time in another place, completely different weather prevailed, but it had never occurred to him that one only had to pierce the thin cloud cover in order to penetrate into this area of endless, bright blue.

The man's pale eyes rest on her expectantly for a moment, then he abruptly turns away again, pressing his head into the small cushion attached to the back of the seat. What are you reading? he asks with a brusque gesture of his hand toward the sheets of paper lying on the folded-down little table in front of her. His nervous reaction to the sun, his sensitivity to light, did not prepare her for the definite, almost commanding tone in which he addresses the question to her. He sits there with his eyes closed, audibly breathing in and out; in response to her question as to whether he feels sick, he shakes his head in a way that could mean anything.

She notices that no one is talking on this flight: the passengers have put their sweaters or their inflatable neck pillows around their shoulders and gone to sleep a few minutes after takeoff, their glasses, their in-flight magazines and tablets on standby still in their hands, which are now slowly relaxing and opening.

You don't have to answer the question—her neighbor now says softly, almost in a whisper, as if he were suffering from great and incalculable pain—excuse the indiscretion. Without opening his eyes, he reaches into the small travel bag at his feet, pulls out a tattered copy of Madame Bovary, *and places it in his lap, as if he could foresee the end of this condition that seems to have come over him so suddenly, as if he's preparing for a later time that will be devoted to reading, although the flight is already nearing its end.*

She is on her way to a conference on the French Atlantic coast, a four-day gathering of writers from the European Union, some Balkan countries, Algeria, Cuba, and Brazil, and while she has long been certain that her seatmate is also one of the guests, she knows that the likelihood that he, in turn, will get the idea that she, too, is traveling there is small: one does not suspect a writer in her; she lacks the elegance, the rapturous nature of the lyricist, the flickering eyes of the artist, the cool authority, the eloquence and maturity of the intellectual. She doesn't think ill of her neighbor, of all the older men she mainly meets in these contexts, the literary circles; she mostly believes their incredulous exclamations, the surprise they express when she or other women her age are introduced to them as interlocutors, as colleagues: "How young *you are!" Just as they sometimes fail to notice the crumbs that linger on their lips during the meals they share, those standing receptions. Other things in their environment also seem to escape them easily. And she knows that the vast majority of them, as soon as their attention is called to those crumbs, brush their mouths gratefully as they are embarrassed.*

At the Nantes airport, a chauffeur waits with a sign bearing both their names. Seagulls fly over the parking lot; the writer stands shivering in the still-thin light.

It was quite incomprehensible to him—he says, when they were in the cab driving across the fields toward the ocean—why he accepted the invitation to come here. He knew from experience that these meetings and conferences disrupted his usual way of functioning—that his whole, somewhat finely calibrated existence was thrown into disarray within a very short time and that, for example, in a single moment he lost the ability to take an interest in the cities, these places which were, after all, the very reason for his participation in these events. He instead lay in a kind of torpor in his hotel room, watching television for hours on end, and grew increasingly reluctant to look at himself in the mirrors that were usually placed on the insides of the closet doors, but sometimes also next to the desks, which, incidentally, he never used. During these trips, he had always expended only just enough energy to keep up appearances, while inwardly he was disintegrating. He appeared for breakfast, neatly dressed, and had conversations over coffee about contemporary literature,

*the plight of the feuilleton, or mutual acquaintances in
Berlin; then he went back to his room—undressing and
lying down and sleeping or watching television and eating cookies until he was ready for his next performance
or the next meal with the group and dressed again and
left the room.*

*She responds to his questions about what she's do-
ing, what she is dealing with; for a while now she has
been claiming to friends that she's been working on a
book about love, and as a rule the friends reacted with
laughter, as if she had made a good joke, and she herself also laughed when she talked about it. Until now
she had stayed away from these things—love, feelings,
sex—and this decision had been to her advantage in a
certain way: she often received praise for the fact that
the spectrum of her so-called "topics" was not limited
to what women supposedly usually worked on, but also
included the historical-political, or questions about and
a vocabulary of technology. Her work was character-
ized above all by the fact that it bore the hallmarks of a
literature that was seen as male, although it came from
the hand of a woman, because, she says with a laugh,
she had come to her senses in spite of her gender, rejected the weepiness of women, and changed sides. The
writer leans forward to look between the front seats at
the landscape ahead of them.*

*When he enters the foyer of the conference building late
in the evening that same day, she has been talking to
an Austrian translator for some time: he talks at length
about a trip through divided Germany that he made as*

210

a twenty-year-old student with a poet who later gained some renown, but whose career unfortunately came to an abrupt end when his publisher gambled away his relatively modest fortune in the course of a single night at a casino here on the French Atlantic coast—at the casino in Quiberon—and the publishing house ceased to exist overnight.

Pacific oysters are carried in on glass plates, shimmering silver, sharp-edged mussels. The German cultural attaché claps his hands in delight.

When the translator excuses himself, she remains alone at her high table, and as the voices of those present bang up against her as if she were a stick—a pipe that someone hammered into the sandy bottom of the Atlantic off the coast—she opens the shells of the mussels and drips the juice of a lemon onto the meat, which she then removes from its shell and lets slide into her mouth with her head tilted slightly back.

Here's what her neighbor from the plane says as he sits next to her: "If you consider that women throughout time have read novels, novels, *which were above all about love: the rescue by the lover, the abduction in a carriage, the princes who rode in on elegant horses to take the women. And if one also considers that this reading has always been derogatorily evaluated for seducing and distracting the female reader by making her vain and impairing her sense of reality, then—he says—one might conclude that it is a form of escapism cultivated over the centuries and up to the present day—a retreat into, even if only imagined, private pleasure. But just as likely, he continues, this practice of reading could perhaps be understood as something important handed down from one generation to the next: a potential, the utopia of overcoming certain* divides, *or the refusal to acknowledge them at least.*

But good, yada yada, *he says after a short pause.*

Later, when she steps through a small glass door onto the balcony of the building, already tired, she sees the writer standing next to a woman who explains that it is surely impossible to overlook the fact that it is capital that has an interest in pitting those it exploits against each other, dividing them and urging them to compete for their place in this order imposed on them. The writer raises his hand in greeting when he sees her—the young woman from the plane—and tells her to come closer, while at the same time he follows the remarks of the woman next to him, nodding. Yes, yes, he says, she is certainly right, and in a certain sense they—he and this young woman from Switzerland—both touched on this question earlier when they were talking about love, hadn't they?

Ooh la la says the woman and strokes the writer's upper arm. He laughs the way he laughed hours before at the stable blue, at the light of the tropopause.

At night: the view from the window of the hotel of escalators leading up from the street directly into the interior of a shopping center now in darkness.

Early in the morning she walks to the coast; the beach is smooth and empty. In the distance she can see the upper floors and the large chimneys of the cruise ships that are built in this place. Hence the Poles—the president of the local literary society had said to her, after inquiring about her opinion of the Nouveau Roman—*if you pay attention, you will see on every corner the* establishments, *the snack bars, frequented by the Polish shipyard workers.*

In the breakfast room of the Holiday Inn, the artistic director of the conference waves her over. Sit down with us, will you? You can read later. She comes and sits at the table with her coffee cup, papers, and pencil in her hands. And is everything okay, room, housekeeping, did you sleep well, yes, very nice. Next to him, her neighbor from the plane is having breakfast; with slightly reddened eyes and damp hair he sits there and is silent. Every now and then he smiles briefly, as if he were following the conversation of some invisible companion.

*When asked again what she is reading, she says it is a version of the so-called Inkle and Yarico story; the director shakes his head—*doesn't ring a bell—*as the writer cracks an egg.*

After the first few pages, she had already known that she was, in principle, facing another Robinsonian escapade: Europeans hurrying over islands, farmers sitting in their armchairs, drinking bitter coffee and studying Kästner's History of Mathematics, *explorers, priests, and soldiers who, for all of the things in these places*

213

they considered the "New World," *had only brought their language, their preconceived notions—incompatible instruments.*

The text and its vocabulary bored her, but perhaps in the subordinate clauses and between the lines, she thought she might be able to find something after all: a detail as a gate that would lead out into a less clear-cut but more realistic historical reality; passages pointing to experiences and circumstances that were more complicated than their recorders would have us believe.

Inkel—she says to the director and the writer sitting in front of his egg—Inkel was on the run, his feet carried him out of the sight of the savages, *and he was hiding desperately in the dark bushes, when suddenly a girl appeared, an* orange-red girl, *barely clothed, and Inkel begged for her help:* take me as your slave *he begged her, and* give me life by the sweetness of your voice, and its sweeter contents.

She, Yariko, looked at the European, whom she did not understand, and then said in her language that obviously he belonged to the enemies, to those who came rowing in their flying boats, *bringing death and destruction with them, but now he seemed to need urgent help, and* whoever you are: *she will take care of him. She gave him fruit, and while he ate she ran her hand through his hair.*

Later she left him in a safe place, but every day she came again, and at dusk she sometimes took him to a quiet, deserted ground, where he *fell asleep quite sheltered* by falling waters.

Inkel wanted to take the woman he loved, thought

he loved, with him to Europe; he wanted to dress her in the finest silks and ride around with her in floating houses pulled by horses, *and she in turn wanted to go with him, be his companion forever, and despite the circumstances, it was a happy time they spent together, and when they saw a ship, they boarded it.*

When the author from Havana enters the breakfast room, the director raises his hand in greeting: they say you were the last to leave the hotel bar yesterday, but it doesn't seem possible, how old are you, by the look of you you can't be more than twenty. The woman laughs and clasps her hair at the nape of her neck.

They board the ship, and then what, asks her neighbor from the plane later, when they meet again in the lobby, his hair still damp. Oh, I see, she says.

The ship was a slave ship on its way to Barbados, and when it arrived, the owners of the sugar mills came running: they needed the slaves to produce their sugar cheaply. When Inkel saw how great the demand was, his merchant spirit, which had been asleep until then, spoke up again, *and he offered the woman who was traveling with him to a Barbadian farmer.*

Yariko begged Inkel not to do it or at least to take her as a slave himself, even more so because she was pregnant, but Inkel was determined, and the prospect of a child allowed him to raise the price.

In a second part—says the woman from the plane, when they are already approaching the conference building — Yariko is released by her buyer, and Inkel, who by now regrets everything, is punished for his heartlessness with slave labor, but at some point he is told that someone has paid for his emancipation.

Yariko, the writer says, hands buried in his coat pockets.

Later she sees him, the writer, walking alone across the pier; unnoticed by him some birds fly over his head.

If you leave the conference hall through the rear exit and go through the next unlabeled door, he says to her, you enter the adjacent hall, where there's a market to-day, rows of stalls selling fried plantains, chicken stew, and fufu, woven blankets and carved figures. Unlike here, it was very warm there, he says. He had imme-diately gotten lost, wandering between the stalls, and bought earrings for an acquaintance, a friend.

When she goes back to the waterfront before she leaves, she remembers the long corridors of the ferry on which she sailed from Venice to Patras with her family when she was eleven years old, the extensive system of corri-dors and staircases, the abandoned cars far below, the constant ringing of the slot machines from somewhere.

—

Thursday, Aarau: As I step from the underpass onto the street, I stand in front of the former *Café Métro / Playland*. On a windowpane the image of the machines

SPUTNIK, SUPER-BALL 500, SPUTNIK JACKPOT, CHERRY BALL.

Swiss Plateau.

In the Ringier Bildarchiv (RBA): negative bags, pencil cases, an envelope (RBA 6 Werner BRUNI) with prints. The archivist hands me white gloves: Here is the switch for the light console, then I'll leave you to it.

Thursday, May 2, 1979
   Millionaire Lotto winner Werner Bruni (taller man with coat no tie) with his boss Walter Hauenstein, who will manage his money at his request.

Seven pictures of Bruni and Hauenstein shaking hands in the boss's office. The lighting wasn't good: in some photographs, the men appear to be standing in the dark; in others, their white, overexposed faces are almost contourless.

The picture that was finally printed on the front page of the newspaper on May 3, 1979, shows Hauenstein beaming at the camera, while Bruni turns to his employer as if looking up at him, enthusiastically and with admiration, although he is much taller, the lottery ticket in both of his hands. It seems to be evening; at least, there's a reflection of the ceiling lamp in the window.

—

The more I think I know about this story, the more numerous the discrepancies, deviations: Times, numbers, formulations that contradict each other indicate that the memories are faulty, the research inaccurate, or the dating can be wrong. And because the video reporter, the BLICK photographer, the journalist, the lotto king, and his ghostwriter quote each other and rely on each other's accounts, on each other's reports, there is no actual narrative, no *true incident*, no reliable source to go back to: The story of the Lotto King begins with the appearance of the photographers.

But this initiation, this first reception, *the making of a king* on the top floor of the Rebell ski factory is already questionable:

The dates I find in the archive do not coincide with the sequence of events in WB's memory or with what the ghostwriter noted, and the photographer whose name I find on the back of a print showing the king and the chief that evening writes from Steffisburg that he did not work for the newspaper at all in the year in question, 1979.

So, it's as if everything could always have been different just as easily: just as the carriage that transports Louverture through France in the summer of 1802 suddenly becomes two in the sources.

On that evening, which may have been a Tuesday, but more likely a Wednesday, the two had apparently already declared that the boss would take care of his employee's lottery winnings from now on:

It is quite possible that he only wants the best for his subordinate, who knows nothing about money and how to handle it,

no idea,

it's also possible that he's not quite sure of the new king after all: like a plant that shot up overnight,

Ghost Plant,

so thin and tall and very white in the flash.

—

A second picture: WB and his wife in the living room. In front of them, blurred, a fruit bowl; in the background hanging plants, built-in shelving; above the shelves a stretched fox fur. It is the year 1979.

Only when I have long since put the photo aside do they appear to me: at the two far ends of the uppermost shelf of the living room stand the two figurines from the auction—the one on the left with her arms raised above her head, on the right the one carrying a vessel on her shoulder. Between them is a neatly arranged and labeled collection of stones, two decorated containers, a globe.

The whole apartment was filled with objects and souvenirs—here a camel, there a long-necked jug. On the walls were a picture of a sailing ship, two crossed knives; and on the TV next to a vase of flowers were two more black figurines, both standing, one of them carrying a spear and shield, a warrior. They shine brightly on the negatives, as if they were created from fluorescent fabrics, as if only photography could reveal them.

Everything went under the auction hammer in 1986, writes WB or his ghostwriter, even the sculptures he got in Haiti. But the picture says: In 1979 the two figures are already in this living room, five years before the lottery king even began his Caribbean journey.

—

Before the 1979 stroke of luck: vacations in Tunisia, Morocco, Romania; three times he travels to Kenya with his wife.

"In Kenya, she preferred to lounge in a deck chair, napping or looking out onto the pool with a drink in her hand. I was drawn away. To the animals in the wilderness and to the Maasai with their herds. The black man never did anything to me. But R. was scared. Rightly so. Against her, the proud warriors would have turned the tables." (*Lotto King*, p. 70)

Maybe they are from there, from Kenya, the figurines, the women and the warrior, the wooden vessels, the knives on the wall.

—

A third picture shows the auction in Spiez. The picture's caption: "Lotto millionaire Bruni: The auctioneer tries to bring wine to the man at Werner Bruni's auction." Behind the auctioneer, holding a wine bottle in his right hand, a sound engineer with headphones and a microphone who must have been part of the documentary filmmaker's team.

I already knew, of course, that the stories were fabricated, that memories can't be relied on. I told you I didn't sleep in school.

—

A week after BLICK reveals his identity, the lottery king is once again on the front page on May 10, 1979: "1 million in taxes—he's left with 729,386…"

In the same issue (p. 11) an article about the bandleader Teddy Stauffer (70): For seven days he celebrated his birthday on the beaches of Acapulco, a chef from Biel set up a huge buffet for his birthday, and the Arriaga family played Mexican music. Fireworks. Afterward, he went to the Mexican mountains with his "new, dark-skinned girlfriend, Jewel." (27)

A picture: "Teddy Stauffer with his new girlfriend Jewel on the king size bed in the Super Isla Villa: It was big love at first sight!"

Also on p. 11: job advertisements for an oil-fired fitter, electricians, an insulation technician and an insulation installer.

In the left column, the image of a dancer:

From Haiti
May 4–13 in Zurich, Züspa Halls
Ballet Bacoulou:
An exotic show with ravishing rhythms.
Colorful, fascinating.
22 male and female dancers.
Unique to film and photograph
[...]
at the Photoexpo

Port Salute

– So Port Salute was the happy time?

– In the book about his life, the life of the country's first lottery millionaire, it says: "Haiti is my most beautiful memory." When he thinks of his lost wealth, he thinks of Haiti, and there was not much more left for him than a shell the children fetched from far out at sea, a big, delicate, pink shell. Clearly, perhaps just spin coming from the reporter, the ghostwriter: this brief, beautiful, strange flight of fancy before downfall inexorably takes its course. The shiny seashell as a sign that the worker as king was briefly elsewhere, that he flew somewhere he liked, where he felt quite at home. That it was this island of all places—yes, that's strange, but then again it makes sense to me.

Just recently I was thinking about how, during winter on the French coast, in the icy wind, I saw Polish workers assembling the cruise ships, those huge vehicles that will then—at some point in the future—anchor, for example, in northern Haiti, in Labadee, where a cruise company runs a private paradise for its guests. It's a leased beach area separated by fences from the rest of the island. The question of what these Polish men have to do with the people on the island, its inhabitants, is in fact far too simple, but then it quickly becomes complicated.

In the case of WB, I can't make up my mind either, whether he was not a master after all too, friendly, but in the end striding across the island as a master. Whether he saw himself as a patron, or whether he really felt that something connected him to this place, that he was drawn to the people as if he had lived a previous life there, as if he was returning to a place of significance, as if he had seen it all in a dream once.

—

Why not invent everything, when even the *true story* is obviously a fiction, or a montage at the very least.

The invention of the *happy time*: The Fairy Tale of X in Luck.

—

It is still dark when the plane leaves Basel-Mulhouse airport for Paris. The fields next to the tarmac covered with snow: it has been snowing for hours, for days maybe. One of the passengers, a tall, slender man—X— took one more look at the thermometer before he left his house at two o'clock in the morning to drive to the airport: six degrees below zero. Now he sits there with his back straight as the plane climbs steeply and, eventually, reaches its cruising altitude: he won't leave this cabin for sixteen hours. For quite some time it remains dark outside the windows; then light comes, and the plane is perhaps already over the Atlantic. The year 1984 is not yet forty hours old.

When the orange signal above the rows goes out and the passengers are allowed to leave their seats, the man stands up, takes off his thick jacket, and places it carefully folded in the compartment above him. Now and then over the next few hours he exchanges a couple sentences with the people to his right and left, with whom he seems to have a connection, but mostly he remains silent and looks ahead without saying anything, without looking for something to busy himself with. Flying interests him, but not too terribly either; after all, this isn't the first time he's been on a plane—he's already flown to Hammamet in Tunisia, to visit North Africa more generally, and he's been to Kenya three times.

Just as a conversation develops about the course of the time zones and the movement the plane is making at this moment—backward in time, but forward with the sun, the electrician next to him wagers—he closes his eyes. He doesn't want to join in this affable chatter right now, not yet: he'll have to spend plenty of time in the company of this small group of his countrymen and women. In his mind's eye, he sees the light spreading continuously westward across the globe, sees a hand lightly nudging the table globe in his living room and causing it to rotate, sees communication conduits, construction sites—indeed, construction site after construction site; then he falls asleep again.

Twice, first in Paris and then on the other side of the Atlantic, in Guadeloupe, the plane lands and spends some time on the ground. Ultimately, it touches down in Port-au-Prince. X, jacket over his arm, steps out of the *plane behind the electrician and onto the stairs leading down to the tarmac. He thinks he is going to die: the heat has an instant grip on his body, it clutches him, still wearing the same clothes in which he had stepped out of the house into snow flurries at two o'clock in the morning Central European time. So suddenly and completely does he find himself enveloped in this burning heat that for a moment he actually seems to lose his sight and hearing: he can just barely make out the out-line of the electrician's girlfriend who exited the plane before him. Her white skin shines so brightly in the sun that it almost reminds him, X, of cold again, the cold light of a welding torch. The electrician shields his eyes with his hand. Behind X, the floor layer steps out of the plane, cursing: Damn, sweltering heat here. Then his wife, the floor-layer's wife, sunglasses on a chain around her neck, her arms still holding the lined suede jacket from the European winter. The five of them stag-ger down the stairs and across the blazing tarmac to the airport terminal, while the woman who invited them on this trip—or rather: who hired them and on whose behalf they have thus come here—has already gone on ahead. She, Y, the client, is not experiencing the shock-ing effect of the abrupt changes in climate, the feeling of unreality caused by the artificial lengthening of days, by the delayed nights: she is not impressed, or so it seems.*

Somewhere in the airport the son waves, Y's son, who flew here last year and tried in vain to have the con-tainer that was sent by ship released from the customs warehouse. What a fuss, X thinks wearily, as they stand clustered around the son in front of the terminal: as if he had been missing forever, as if they hadn't seen each other in a zillion years. This cackling, the chattering of the women. He doesn't make a face, just puts his suitcase down after a while, looks around over the others' heads. Later, in the hotel room, he falls asleep immediately.

—

Everything points to autumn again—I say to A., the receiver clamped between the shoulder and ear—fog early in the morning, then later that warm, milky light.

How nice it was to stroll through the heat just a short while ago. A kind of derangement, to slip so blissfully into one's own ruin, isn't it?

—

Erika in the laundry room: Do I have a lot to do today.
    Oh well.   And you, how are you?
    You know how it is.

The feeling that I was hiding things from her: trips taken in secret, joyrides, ghost rides, a last-minute trip to the Caribbean.

Later, her fluttering white sheets in the light of the rising sun. At the Pacchetto kiosk, the lotto jackpot is listed at 8 million.

—

(cont.)

Two days later he's feeling better. He's gotten used to the warmth; instead of his buttondowns he now wears T-shirts; he has also discarded something different, something bigger, with his former clothes. He suddenly seems young, younger, while the heat seems to be getting to the others, giving them extra weight. And now, at last, they leave the capital and cover the 300 kilometers that lie between Port-au-Prince and Port Salute. The artisans, their wives, and X ride in the open bed of the truck among the material from the shipping container: sinks, toilets, a fitted kitchen, hoses, an emergency generator, tools.

No one knows what they saw on the road, those five people in the back of the truck: They hold on to the sides and try to communicate despite the noise of the engine and the lashed cargo; their upper bodies sway simultaneously to the left, then to the right again when one of the trailer wheels hits a pothole. At first they laugh at the way the vehicle rocks over the uneven roadway, but soon they are exhausted by its unpredictable, relentless course. The electrician ties a cloth over his face against the dust so that only his eyes are visible. Not X: he doesn't find that necessary. That's just the way it is here—dusty, period. He's experienced worse.

Indeed: Like Karl Rossmann through Kafka's America, *he seems to be hurled through life—here the baker who smacks him, there his father's bicycle found on the banks of the ice-cold river, or the iron pipes that knock all the teeth out of his mouth at the construction site. Who suspects then, when the tide seems to turn overnight, when the money suddenly rains down on X and they shine the spotlight on him in the TV studios, that he no longer has a single tooth of his own in his mouth.*

In front, next to the driver is Y with her son. Months ago, she told the men about her unusual request: In the Maison Y *in Port-Salut, named after her, pipes have to be laid, toilets connected, wires run, floors laid, and walls painted. X has been recommended to her as a plumber. He thinks about it for a long time, then agrees. He borrows the money for the Air France flight from the bank.*

—

– That's basically what I wanted to say.
– That's all?
– Yes.
– It just occurred to me that you're still wearing the same pants you wore back in the beginning.
– Is that so?
– At that time you claimed you were just standing around in the undergrowth all the time, and I said you would be able to tell by the look of your pants that you had gotten caught on some bushes.
– True fact.
– Would you still say that you're somehow stuck in something?
– Yes, definitely. Right now I'm reading *L'Éducation sentimentale*.

– In there, in that brush or undergrowth?

– Yes, yes. One has to do something.

– Is this your first time reading the book?

– I didn't read all those books. In my family, people tended to go to the movies and read the local newspaper, Dürrenmatt's crime novels, comics, that sort of thing.

– And do you like it, the book?

– Right at the beginning, you know, when the young man, Moreau, boards the ship at Quai Saint-Bernard in Paris and first sees the woman, Madame Arnoux, who will then tie him up for years—when this apparition reveals herself to him for the first time, for a moment a black woman appears there, a nanny, a silk scarf wrapped around her head, whom Arnoux must have "brought back from the islands."

– That's how the book begins?

– Thus begins *L'Éducation sentimentale*.

– I'm a little surprised that you think everything to say has been said now. Especially since the truck hasn't even arrived at its destination.

– I watched it on the internet recently, someone with a camera mounted on the dashboard driving down a winding road to Port Salute and then west along the coast. It must have been shortly after the last hurricane; in any case, there are tree stumps, pale tree skeletons all over the beach, and palm trees that folded up just like that, and it's all very bright, white actually: the sand, the dirt road, the brickwork of the houses that the storm passed over. And then blue sky and the blue of the tarps everywhere where the storm tore off the roofs of the buildings, and one of those houses out there on the coast could certainly be the Swiss woman's villa, which was still just a shell in 1984.

– So the craftsmen who flew in finished the construction?

– Only after they first went to the beach, at least the floor layer and the electrician. They came, after all, from the depths of winter to that sun. Whereas the plumber immediately began working.

– And then?

– If you really think more needs to be told: fine. But if you think there's an end, you're fooling yourself.

—

It must be long after midnight when I wake and walk downstairs: faint light falls through the window openings set into the walls—the first light of the day, I think, creeping up on the horizon. Only when I enter the rooms of the house facing the sea do I hear above the roar of the Atlantic the voices of several people. I step to one of the windows, smell the damp mortar and the water's salt. Outside in the half-light at a long, makeshift table sit Heinrich von Kleist and Adam Smith playing Yahtzee. A little ways off stands the lotto king, his velvet cloak wrapped tightly around his upper body despite the warmth of the night. In the distance, St. Teresa's brothers walk across the beach gathering driftwood for a fire, the wide sleeves of their white shirts flapping in the wind.

—

I'm writing everything now only from memory, swinging myself hand-over-hand from one place that has left its stamp on me while reading to the next: the arrival at the half-constructed shell of the villa, the children who fetch shells from the depths, the thing with the goat.

In addition: my assumptions and second-hand knowledge. From the internet the pictures of clouds, huge white flakes moving across the tropical sky. I invent in my writing the floor-layer's wife's sunglasses and so forth.

All in all, a tinkering project.

—

(*cont.*)

When the truck finally reaches its destination and they jump from the vehicle one after the other over the tailgate, X sees immediately despite the darkness that the building is little more than a sketch, a hint of what will one day in the future nobly be called Maison Y. *They enter the construction site and light candles in order to see. Rats run through the empty rooms. Then they eat and drink, the dust of the journey still in the corners of their eyes, in the creases of their eyelids, in their hair and on sweaty skin. Before them lies the night sea, a dark pool now completely surrounding them: day and night, the waves curl toward the island and break at its edges.*

The next morning, when X steps out of the house, a child stands there boiling water over a fire.

Tall palm trees.

X inspects the construction site, starts installing the toilets and sinks. Whoever tampered with this house before him did a poor job of preparation. The connections of the appliances that X had sent across the Atlantic do not match the installed pipes. But he's familiar with that, the carelessness of others: he'll think of something, he'll make up for his coworkers' sloppiness, and in the end everything will be as it always is—it will be all right. The thermometer registers forty degrees in the shade. He works for hours without a break. His overexertion comes not from a sense of duty, but out of principle.

In the evening when it gets cooler, he goes down to the sea and swims, letting the waves lift him up, wash him about. Afterward, he drinks a glass of rum: that way, he believes, he stays healthy, even when he drinks the coffee of the locals who invite him to their homes, into their huts on the beach. He is disgusted by the coffee they prepare in their meager dwellings, but he accepts the cup or glass that is handed to him anyway, and drinks.

Morning after morning the child carries a bucket of water up to the house and boils it, water for Y.

In the afternoon, when the electrician and the floor installer have long since returned to lying next to their wives on the beach in the glaring sun, other children suddenly stand in the room and eye him, X, and the tools in his hands. They follow him through the rooms, attaching themselves to him. And he tries out his French, which he learned when he worked for the bakers in French-speaking Switzerland, and the children

233

answer, giving their names, French names, all begin-
ning with Jean.

X works persistently on this house, maison Y, which
does not belong to him and never will, and because
nothing seems to escape him—because he seems to
know his way around everything, even those things out-
side his field—he is soon regarded as the foreman: Here
the joints can be made, he says, here the wires have
to be pulled in, here this and this is missing, there's a
problem here.

The foreman on the flat roof with a water hose in his
hand.

Just as he has always given himself over completely to
work on the construction sites of apartment buildings,
hotels, and blocks of condos, he is now giving himself to
this domicile in the Caribbean, even though nothing is
in it for him and even though at home he is the famous
king of the lottery.

—

Just as the workers, according to Marx, bear their own
skin to market: this is what the lottery king seems to
have done in an exemplary manner throughout his life;
indeed, one could say that he offered himself up in an
exceedingly servile manner.

"Nothing was too harsh for me, nothing too dirty."
(p. 37)

In contrast to this, the colleagues who slip away to the Caribbean beach as often as possible. Why should anyone be allowed to ask them to do more than is necessary, since, on the whole, they are already at a disadvantage anyway—i.e., they will never reside between the Tropics of Cancer and Capricorn.

—

In the post office, above the copy machine, is the display of the current lotto jackpot (9.8 million). I make copies of literature, texts, questions: "Was the Plantation Slave a Proletarian?" Outside, a bright confusion, traffic near standstill; pedestrians heave their purchases between cars across the street. The bus drivers stand at the bus stop, their hands in the pockets of their dark blue pants.

—

If people asked what I thought of him, the lottery king, I would be embarrassed:
     An ordinary man,
     simple worker,
     a so-called loser,
     the loser as the winner/a winner who lost everything,

a melancholic, with bright, piercing eyes,

stupid, the way he talked about women.

(With the exception of Heidi Abel, who received him in the TV studio back then: *a superwoman*.)

—

In the films about WB are some photographs from his private collection: the finished bath in the vacation home, palm trees, palm trees before sunset, children climbing the trunks of palm trees, WB and the goat.

—

(*cont.*)

When asked how he's doing, he nods: Thank you, good. He has gotten used to the climate. He drinks a glass of rum twice a day. That a whole ocean lies between him and his wife relieves him. At least that's how he would have described it: in principle he has always preferred to be alone.

Now the children keep him company, jumpy creatures who lie on the floor to watch him handle the wrench, who appear suddenly next to him on the flat roof, in the laundry room, on the beach, where they carry large pink shells toward him as if offering sacrifices.

After weeks, once the house takes clearer and clearer shape, Y hosts a party. The butcher delivers sausages, and the children bring their parents from the surrounding countryside. They all want to see the house, the small miracles X and his colleagues have accomplished, now that the connections fit on the pipes and electric light shines from the ceilings in all the rooms.

X explains things in his baker's French, and everyone cheers, hanging on his every word. He looks out into the crowd of guests around him: They are cheering me on, he says to himself, they are celebrating me. Nothing in his face betrays the realization, and he continues with the tour of the house, explaining everything as best he can: The only thing missing here is a water supply. L'amenée de l'eau.

Late night: Y walks across the veranda with small, prancing steps and toasts the remaining guests with her glass. She is happy: the worst is over. Her colleagues are sitting on a bench drinking beer. One of them points with his chin to the Caribbean Sea. That cursed roaring. It could drive you crazy. They laugh. But let the sun shine on your dome every day, while the others freeze their fingers off at home: Why not?

X stands up and takes a few steps: he doesn't need any more of this talk now; what he actually likes is the relative silence at night, the total darkness.

Then a man detaches himself from a group of people around the fire. It is the site manager, who comes over to him and immediately gets to the point: whether he might not want to stay. In the distance, the movement of the palm's dark fronds, as if beckoning him.

Of course he can't stay. A few weeks later, he flies back across the big pond, *as he calls it, that huge, light-blue pool of water.*

—

WB packs his tools and flies back across the Atlantic. He has a farewell gift, a machete, sent to him by mail.

He tells his ghost writer that he made a crutch out of a branch for a man who was missing a foot and left some money to his child and two others for uniforms, shoes, notebooks, and school fees for three years, etc.

For that, he got the machete, which came in a braided sheath.

—

And from the Caribbean, it is said elsewhere, the two figures also came, the sculptures that—two years later when the king's beautiful cloak is taken off and the crown removed from his head—are auctioned for thirty-five francs in Spiez.

As if the two bright shadows—already visible on the shelf in WB's living room on the negatives from 1979/80—were messengers from the future. Signs. Also: as if they prematurely announced the end.

He probably brought them with him back from Kenya, where he was drawn away from the pool, out into the plains, into the so-called wilderness.

—

His colleagues after his return: Has it come so far now that we get *a N——* as a co-worker.

He's so tan you'd think he'd been on vacation all winter, sleeping in the sun while those who stayed here tramped through the mud to the construction sites day after day.

In reality he worked for weeks—at least that's what his book says, for free, *gratis*, and even paid for the flight himself,

> that he didn't indulge himself much,
> except for the goat:
> You can't tell by looking at him.

—

The dethronement of the king begins the following year. He had already withdrawn his boss's power of attorney over his account a few years earlier because he wanted to take matters into his own hands. He has long since sold the twelve-plex—out of which one resident after another has moved—at the price he paid for it (1.95 million).

WB and his wife lose track of things: they are doing all this for the first time. The pile of unpaid bills is growing into the five-, six-figure range.

Then, on August 2, 1986, the headline: "First Swiss lottery millionaire in bankruptcy!" The debts, it says, amounted to 670,000 francs. The day before, a national holiday, the opening of bankruptcy proceedings were announced in the *Simmentaler Gazette*.

—

And so the auction: the men, women, and children who stream into the hall of the inn on the Thunersee to see the possessions of the fallen king. Expectantly they sit at the long tables, stand crowded outside in the hallway, waiting for the beginning of the ritual that will finally teach this cocky laborer a lesson and restore order.

All eyes are on the auctioneer, who assumes the role of master of ceremonies: a priest with wine bottles, a karabiner rifle in his hands.

Then the two figurines, the two female figures made of wood or brightly polished stone that previously stood on WB's shelf.

Who's bidding?

Just look at those breasts

(*laughter*)

—

In Flaubert: The auction of Madame Arnoux's clothes after her husband's bankruptcy as a ghastly "distribution of her relics."

—

Assumption: The worker, the gambler, this short-lived king, is in no way assumed to have bought the pieces for pleasure—i.e., to have possessed and exhibited them as objects of his lust—because that would, at minimum, mean conceding to him potency and sovereignty. His losses, the bankruptcy would be almost laudable under these circumstances: the consequence of his unreasonable, greedy, deliberate actions.

Rather, on this day, one laughs at the figurines to show that one has understood something that the simpleton missed entirely. Like a child, he put them in the living room, the two women, because he thought they were beautiful, and they reminded him of a pleasurable time; he never touched them (so to speak); he fell asleep harmlessly on the sofa beneath them.

Not even this, according to the insinuation, could he manage: instead of dominating them, he leaned (fraternally) toward them, let them shelter him,

and so crossed the gulf with just one foot.

—

– Do you yourself believe that this is what happened?
– Well, no.
– But what then?
– Complicated, I think it was complicated. Different things were happening at the same time. He probably didn't know exactly what it was about those figurines and what it meant to drag them home, those women and the warriors, and then put them on his television. And even if he felt a closeness—if the sculptures had reminded him not only of package tours and the white beaches of the Antilles, but of friends, of relationships—that would have been utterly presumptuous, even ridiculous. He certainly seems to have made friends, but then there is also the story with the goat, for instance.
– Another goat?

– A young goat "with two beautiful little horns," to quote him.

—

Bruni on the animal, (p. 109):
"I bought it from the dealer for eight dollars. For this I also got a rope so that I could lead it home. At home I put an old coconut mat under a papaya tree, collected grass, brought it water."

—

(*cont.*)

Even as he took his seat on the plane that would take him back to Europe, X thought of the goat, the animal for which he had paid eight dollars. What had he been thinking, Y had asked him the previous evening, when he was sitting on the veranda drinking a beer. After all, a goat like that couldn't just be carted around anyway.

X orders red wine, drinks without joining in the others' conversations, and watches as the flight attendants prepare the cabin for the night. He looks at their braided hair, the light braids from which fine strands are coming loose in some places.

Why shouldn't he have bought it, the little animal that so willingly pattered along beside him: a whole live goat for eight dollars. The watery, alert eyes, like she's always laughing. And how funny when she drinks, isn't it (slurp, slurp).

The gurgling laughter of the children.

*He had not expected, even if his colleagues and Y unan-
imously said that it was only a matter of time, that he
would at some point, perhaps one evening, get out of the
warm sea, having let the spray whirl about his feet for
a while and then, still on the way back to* Maison Y, *see
that the goat was no longer there.*

*Now that he's on the plane, he accompanies himself
once again on that walk, in search of the animal. How
he follows this or that path, walking through the ev-
er-oppressive heat, his ankles and calves covered in
sand, and then sees the slaughtered goat lying there.
Someone is bending over it at that moment, putting it on
a tray. Someone is preparing a lemon marinade. They
have cut off its head.*

*X on that path in the darkness. The blood of the goat a
black pool on the dusty ground. Above him the crowns
of the palms swaying ominously now. He crosses his
arms in front of his chest, but otherwise does not move:
stands there with his head slightly tilted to the side and
watches how the goat is treated, how it is prepared. He
says nothing, not even when people spot him and wave
to him as if it were no big deal, as if they wanted to invite him to join them for the meal. He remains standing
without reacting to their gesticulation until they turn
back to the animal, murmuring softly.*

—

How he reacts in reality, WB, when he discovers the goat, is not clear from his memoirs, the ghostwriter's notes.

There is only the comment that the people (the locals), who earned a dollar a day from him at the building site, would immediately go gamble it away at the cock fights.

That they then offered him the skin of the goat to buy.

They were all terribly poor.

—

– That's your end of the story of the lotto king?
– I don't know. I would like to let him ascend at the end, let him ascend into the heavenly firmament, so to speak, into the blue tropopause, let him leave from there, out of this confusion. The great letting go of all things, and in the end, ecstasy.

—

Now, revise everything once again: Return to each thing one last time—hold them up to the light, question them.

At Letzigraben, two people on a stroll picking the overripe cherries from the trees.

Natalie leaning against her bike, waiting.

Remember when Peter arrived and talked about *Synchronicity*?

—

So walk once again through the place where everything is gathered, everything I have come across lately: the landscapes, landmarks, buildings like makeshift backdrops pushed together. Between them the props and relics, the witnesses, witnesses of secret rites, objects of desire:

The figures in the hands of the auctioneer,

the two candles the boy has carried through the gardens of the sanatorium, the wax running down their sides has been cooling for some time,

a slice of bread from the cupboard of the hungry,

my aunt's Twingo as it stood in front of a restaurant on Lake Constance,

half a dozen carriages,

a golden arrow,

the conductor's stick,

sugar (fields, mountains, cubes)

...

—

My mother says on the phone (September 9) that she had once stood in the sanatorium garden as a child, but she did not remember entering any of the buildings. Nor does she remember who accompanied her there.

—

On the internet: The son of the owner of the house in Haiti today sells water on the island —

Eau Miracle®
Eau potable de première qualité
traitée par osmose inverse

– Moi je bois Eau Miracle, et vous?

—

*Between the steep walls of the furrowed coast I descend
to the sea, sweat running down my face in streams.
Young men, wearing nothing except their swim trunks,
dusty sneakers, and a towel wrapped around their necks,
overtake me at a run. Later, I see them again down on
the beach: with a few steps of a run-up, they plunge from
the cliffs into the blue water, ten, twenty meters deep.
Far out, white daysailers sail toward the Côte d'Azur.
I lie for hours with my eyes closed on the sandy ground
under the pine trees, and at some point I fall asleep.*

*When the bay is already half in shade, one of the cliff
divers suddenly appears next to me. Wet pants cling
to his thin legs; his upper body is long and lean and
tanned. He has collected these papers, he says, which
obviously slipped out of my hand while I was sleeping
and were then scattered by the wind. He hands me a
messy stack of crumpled copies—M. F. K. Fisher's record of the meals she ate on an Atlantic passage in 1932.
Even before departure, at the Vieux Port of Marseille,
she notes a bouillabaisse, then, aboard the small Italian
cargo ship, the* Feltre, *Italian cheese, salami, fruit. Veal.
Heavy, rough wines. Weeks later in Central American
ports, she will eat cool, soft papayas and green oranges;*

drink dark yellow wines; savor the milk of coconuts as if intoxicated; she will be handed avocados and small bowls of cooked fruit.

Like a Renaissance painting—she writes—is the long table on deck of the captain's evening meal, with pies, grapes, two stuffed pheasants. At the end, after the passengers have applauded the ship's cook, a sudden silence falls. Slowly, three kitchen boys appear, laboriously lifting something up the stairs, a thing of the greatest strangeness, which now presents itself to the eyes of the passengers, swaying: a replica of the Cathedral of Milan spun entirely out of sugar; the dusty and repeatedly repaired masterpiece of the ship's cook.

Only Germans, says the cliff diver, come here to read. I watch him squeeze his sandy feet into his sneakers without untying the laces or using his hands. They come with big backpacks, the Germans, and cook things on their gas stoves. Sausages. That I only had this pathetic bag and these papers with me was uncharacteristic. The cliff diver laughs. He uses the formal form when addressing me.

Sprechen Sie Deutsch?

Vous faites quoi, ici?

I wanted to stop working on something but didn't know how, I say. It seemed easier to just get away. The cliff diver nods with his eyebrows drawn together: You left without quitting your job. In the broadest sense, yes. Something like that.

He laughs, satisfied, and hangs his towel in the bushes to dry.

Last night, when he came home feeling just crazy, he saw the police standing a few meters in front of his house, by a small field. The neighbors often put their junk there— broken vacuum cleaners, broken children's cars, CD towers, that kind of thing—and usually the things are gone the next day. But when he arrived last night, he saw that someone had put all their furniture out there, all the stuff, everything that belonged in an apartment. And the policemen went around with their flashlights among the upholstered furniture, and there were still things on the shelves of the furniture: knickknacks, ugly bowls. He had parked his moped to take a closer look at this scene, and the three of them stumbled around in this ghost apartment, c'était chelou, *it was really weird.*

The cliff diver beats himself with the right hand on his narrow, brown chest, as if admonishing himself not to stand around here any longer. Then he lets his gaze wander over the bay, and when he spots a friend who has been striding irresolutely along the edge of a cliff for a while, he bursts into a loud howl, hopping from one leg to the other and throwing his arms in the air as if he were representing an animal, as if he were imitating a ridiculous bird with wings too large for its body.

Jump, you rotten egg.

Then he abruptly turns back to me. And you like it here, in these bushes, he asks, yes? He points to the dry brambles with his sneaker. What can I say to that? You can say whether you like it, the underbrush. He looks at me with expressionless eyes, waiting for an answer. Breaks the branches of the bushes between his fingers. Out in front of the bay, a motorboat pulls a water skier in ever tighter circles over the sea. I point to a tear in my pants. On the way here I got caught on a bush. He shrugs: It happens.

Far above our heads on the steep slope the cliff diver's friends are returning to town. Two or three times they pause briefly and wave to him. He pulls the towel from the bushes and places it around his neck. So, he says then, impatiently, as if he had been obliged against his will to take care of this pale woman and her papers. Can you find your way back on your own? I say: Just up, up and up, and then, at the highest point, left into the woods. The cliff diver sways his head back and forth skeptically. Not quite. But somehow you'll find your way out again, he says, and walks away.

Good luck.

I watch him as he walks away from the sea on the bright, dusty path. Arms wheeling, he climbs steeply upward toward the glistening sun.

Sources

Unless otherwise noted, quotations by and about Ellen West are taken from Ludwig Binswanger's case study *Der Fall Ellen West: Eine anthropologisch-klinische Studie* (*The Case of Ellen West: An Anthropological-Clinical Study*) in the Swiss Archives for Neurology and Psychiatry Volumes LIII, LIV, and LV, Zurich 1944/45.

Heinrich von Kleist's *Die Verlobung in St. Domingo* (*The Betrothal in St. Domingo*) is quoted from the revised edition, Stuttgart 2000.

The passages on Teresa of Ávila are based on the German translation *Das Buch meines Lebens Vol. 1* of her *El libro de la vida* (*The Life of Saint Teresa of Ávila by Herself*) translated and edited by Ulrich Dobhan and Elisabeth Peeters, Freiburg 2001. With designated exceptions, all quotations by and about Teresa of Ávila are taken from this edition.

The story of lottery winner Werner Bruni is told in Bruni's *Lottokönig: Einmal Millionär und zurück* (*Lotto King: Once a Millionaire and Back Again*), Gockhausen 2010, and two documentaries by Christoph Müller: *Gegenspieler – Die furchtbare plötzliche Freiheit* (*Opponent – The Terrible Sudden Freedom*), 1980, and *Der König und sein Chef* (*The King and His Boss*), 1987. They serve as important sources for the book.

13 Hunger was ... the chaos. *The Dream Songs* by John Berryman, New York 1991, p. 333.

13 Urge ... Infatuation, etc. *Über die Liebe: Meditationen* (*On Love: Aspects of a Single Theme*) by José Ortega y Gasset and translated from Spanish by Helene Weyl with the collaboration of Fritz Ernst, Stuttgart 1933, p. 157.

16 like a poplar on a swollen river. *Biographien der Wahnsinnigen* (*Biographies of the Insane*) by Christian Heinrich Spiess, Darmstadt 1976, p. 241.

16 He left ... me up! Ibid., p. 269.

21 with two ... to let. *Orte: Aufzeichnungen* (*Places: Notes*) by Marie Luise Kaschnitz, Frankfurt 1975, p. 64.

22 as if to want ... not what. *Die allmähliche Verfertigung der Idee beim Schreiben* (*The Gradual Finishing of the Idea in Writing*) by Hermann Burger, Frankfurt Lecture on Poetics, Frankfurt 1986, p. 72.

22 Or places ... all over. *Orte*, Kaschnitz, p. 8

24 I will ... and cried. *Tagebücher* (*Diaries*) by Waslaw Nijinsky, Frankfurt 1998, p. 46f.

24 the orderlies ... as midwives. *Radetzkymarsch* (*Radetzky March*) by Joseph Roth, Kolo 1978, p. 217.

24 spoiled madmen ... rich families. *Radetzkymarsch*, Roth, p. 217.

25 And quickly ... in the spaceship. In *Marie Luise Kaschnitz: Eine Biographie* (*Marie Luise Kaschnitz: A Biography*) by Dagmar von Gersdorff, Frankfurt 1991, p. 9.

26 From time ... eat something first. In *Ellen West: Gedichte, Prosatexte, Tagebücher, Krankengeschichte* (*Ellen West: Poems, Prose Texts, Diaries, Case Histories*) edited by Naamah Akavia and Albrecht Hirschmüller, Kroning 2007, p. 56.

29 The night ... happened next. *Things I Don't Want to Know: On Writing* by Deborah Levy, London 2014, p. 25.

30 a terrible ... of a web. "Das dicke Kind" ("The Fat Child") in *Lange Schatten* (*Long Shadows*) by Marie Luise Kaschnitz, Hamburg 1960, p. 112.

39 When I ... in danger of sinking. In *Ellen West*, ed. Akavia and Hirschmülller, p. 67.

39 eaten and drunk. *Die männliche Herrschaft* (*Male Domination*) by Pierre Bourdieu and translated from French (*La domination masculine,* 1998) by Jürgen Bolder, Frankfurt 2013, p. 26.

42 It is … must occur. In *Ellen West*, ed. Akavia and Hirschmüller, p. 33.

42 Oh, that … a boy. Ibid., p. 15.

44 at least … too small. *Meine Preise* (*My Prizes*) by Thomas Bernhard, Frankfurt 2009, p. 18.

47 She sat … dusty cretonne. *Dubliner* (*Dubliners*) by James Joyce and translated from English (1914) by Dieter E. Zimmer, Frankfurt 1969, p. 35.

48 I am … of water? In *Ellen West,* ed. Akavia and Hirschmüller, p. 61.

49 And it … In motion … *Lady Chatterley's Lover* by D.H. Lawrence, London 2010, p. 172.

49 with domes … white marble. *Madame Bovary* by Gustave Flaubert and translated from French by Elisabeth Edl, Munich 2018, p. 257.

50 High Sierras … bright grass. "A Left-Handed Commencement Address" by Ursula K. Le Guin, Mills College, Oakland 1983.

52 Since then … energy is diverted. *Die Stunde des Todes* (*The Hour of Death*) by Herbert Achternbusch, Frankfurt 1975, p. 20.

53 O chevalier … his mouth. "Die halbe Birne" ("The Half Pear") by Konrad von Wurzburg (?) in *Novellistik des Mittelalters: Märendichtung* (*Poetics of the Middle Ages: Fairy Tale Poetry*) edited by Klaus Grubmüller, Frankfurt 1996, p. 202.

55 Dust South, Concrete South … Fiction South. "Im Voyagers Apt. 311 East 31st Street, Austin" ("At Voyagers Apt. 311 East 31st Street, Austin") by Rolf Dieter

Brinkmann in *Westwärts 1 & 2 Gedichte* (*Westward 1 & 2: Poems*), Reinbek 1975, p. 79.

57 Mr. Williams … it doesn't. In "The Trial of Edward Gibbon Wakefield, William Wakefield, and Frances Wakefield […]," London 1827, p. 47.

61 the veiled … its pedestal. *Das Kapital, Band 1* (*Capital: Volume 1*) by Karl Marx in *Karl Marx/Friedrich Engels: Werke, Band 23* (*Karl Marx/Friedrich Engels: Collected Works, Vol. 23*), Berlin 1970, p. 787.

65 a storage room … third person. *Übers Eis* (*Over the Ice*) by Peter Kurzeck, Frankfurt 2011, p. 8.

66 the most unhealthy strip … of Brittany. "Freiligrath an Marx, Cologne, 29/7. 49." ("Freiligrath to Marx, Cologne, July 29, 1849") in *Freiligraths Briefwechsel mit Marx und Engels* (*Freiligrath's Correspondence with Marx and Engels*) edited by Manfred Häckel, Germany Academy of Sciences, Berlin 1968, p. 6.

67 Ah, this is … Barbarism. *Im Dickicht von London oder Die Aristokratie und die Proletarier Englands* (*The London Journal of Floral Tristan: The Aristocracy and the Working Class of England*) by Flora Tristan and translated from French (*Promenades dan Londres*, 1840) by Paul B. Kleiser and Michael Pösl, Cologne 1993, p. 88.

69 his original … his plunder. *Facts Relating to the Punishment of Death in the Metropolis* by Edward Gibbon Wakefield, London 1831, p. 22.

73 Unhappy Mr. Peel … Swan River! *Kapital*, Marx, p. 794.

74 I am now … is. "The Trial of Edward Gibbon Wakefield […]," p. 48.

77 Mr. Carr … darkish green. Ibid, p. 81.

77 Did Miss … papa's carriage. Ibid, p. 56.

79 Hyper U … sugar! *Heilige Schrift I* (*Holy Scripture I*) by Wolfram Lotz, unpublished.

85 Determination of first coordinates. *Phänomenologie der Wahrnehmung* (*Phenomenology of Perception*) by Maurice Merleau-Ponty and translated from French (*Phénoménologie de la perception*, 1945) by Rudolf Boehm, Berlin 1966, p. 125.

86 thing like … looked at. "Werfen wie ein Mädchen: Eine Phänomenologie weiblichen Körper Verhaltens, weiblicher Motilität und Raumlichkeit" (*Throwing Like a Girl: A Phenomenology of Female Bodily Behavior, Female Motility, and Spatiality*) by Iris Marion Young, *German Journal of Philosophy* 41 (1993), p. 718.

89 native form … convention allows. *Essais* (*Essays*) by Michel de Montaigne, Zurich 2000, p. 51.

93 uneconomic grasp. *Hegel und Haiti: Für eine neue Universalgeschichte* (*Hegel, Haiti, and Universal History*) by Susan F. Buck-Morss and translated from English (2005) by Laurent Faasch-Ibrahim, Berlin 2011, p. 118.

94 a displacement … for his cousin. Ibid.

95 And I … in America? In *Empire of Cotton: A New History of Global Capitalism* by Sven Beckert, London 2015, p. 82.

96 "Toussaint Louverture and the Slaves of the Bréda Plantations" by David Geggus in *Plantation Societies in the Era of European Expansion* edited by Judy Bieber, Aldershot 1997, p. 275.

97 Prologue … to Haiti. *The Black Jacobins: Toussaint L'Ouverture and the San Domingo Revolution* by C. L. R. James, New York 1989, p. 3.

97 affreuses campagnes … of horror. *Voyage d'un Suisse dans différentes colonies d'Amérique pendant la dernière guerre* (*Voyage to Different American Colonies During the Last War*) by Justin Girod-Chantrans, Neuchâtel 1785, p. 138.

98 Let us … immediately changes. Ibid, p. 332.

98 Eu como tudo. *Eine glückliche Liebe* (*A Happy Love*) by
Hubert Fichte, Frankfurt 1988, p. 23.

102 like … underground of sleep. *Phänomenologie*, Merleau-
Ponty, p. 126.

103 the non-perspective … seen from nowhere. Ibid, p. 91.

103 Body my … I hunt. "Question" in *Poems to Solve* by May
Swenson, New York 1966.

104 Some mud. Concrete. *Die zweite Schuld* (*The Second
Debt*) by Hubert Fichte, Frankfurt 2006, p. 9.

104 and when … that evening. "Bericht des Wirts zum
Stimming Nach E.v. Bülow" ("Report of the innkeeper
Zum Stimming according to E.V. Bülow") in *Heinrich von
Kleist* by C. F. Reinhold, Berlin 1919, p. 258.

108 I don't know … cultivate them. *Voyage à l'Isle de France,
à l'Isle de Bourbon, au Cap de Bonne-Espérance, etc.
avec des observations nouvelles sur la nature et sur les
hommes, Tome premier* (*Voyage to the Island of Mauritius,
Réunion Island, and the Cape of Good Hope, with New
Observations about Nature and People, vol. 1*) by Henri
Bernardin de Saint-Pierre, Amsterdam 1773, p. 201.

108 You are … are sweet. "Zucker" ("Sugar") on *Das rote
Album* (*The Red Album*) by Tocotronic, Berlin 2015.

112 twenty-one days … and sky. *Nijinsky: Der Gott des
Tanzes, biographie* (*Nijinsky: the God of Dance, a
Biography*) by Romola Nijinsky, Frankfurt 1974, p. 211.

113 In any case, … Sanatorium. *Erinnerungen: Erlebte
Psychiatriegeschichte 1920-1960* (*Memories: Lived
History of Psychiatry 1920–1960*) by Max Müller, Berlin
1982, p. 178.

121 We passed … 2 a.m. *Tagebücher aus den Jahren 1936-
1966, Band 2* (*Diaries From the Years 1936-1966*, vol. 2)
by Marie Luise Kaschnitz, Frankfurt 2000, p. 818.

131 single watch manufactory. *Kapital*, Marx, p. 363.

133 I lived … future pain. *Passion simple (Simple Passion)* by Annie Ernaux, Paris 2018, p. 45.

134 Do you... he said. *Trocadero* by Hanna Johansen, Munich 1980, p. 164f.

138 He knows … 11.5.1974. *Montauk* by Max Frisch, Frankfurt 1981, p. 9.

138 "Account of the Montauk Indians, on Long Island (1761)" in *The Collected Writings of Samson Occom, Mohegan: Leadership and Literature in Eighteenth-Century Native America* by Samson Occom and edited by Joanna Brooks, New York 2006, p. 49

142 Sometimes they … always unhurt. Ibid., p. 49.

144 The trail … the palefaces. "Indian Trails: or, Trail of the Montauk" in *The Collected Works of Olivia Ward Bush-Banks* by Olivia Ward Bush-Banks and edited by Bernice F. Guillaume, New York 1991, p. 190.

146 At one point … people here. *Montauk*, Frisch, p. 52.

146 There is … many years. "Pharaoh v. Benson Ruling," New York Supreme Court, October 1910.

148 and when … Whole World. "The Most Remarkable and Strange State Situation and Appearance of Indian Tribes in this Great Continent (1783)" by Samson Occom in *Collected Writings*, p. 58.

149 They dream … four-horse carriage. *Im Dickicht*, Tristan, p. 179.

149 flaming figure … strange fantasy. *Teresa von Avila: Eine leidenschaftliche Seele (Teresa of Ávila: A Passionate Soul)* by Walter Nigg, Zurich 1996, p. 5f, 13.

151 shimmering gems … carved reliquaries. Ibid, p. 22f.

151 Tendencies … the void. Ibid, p. 23.

162 Balzac, when … César Birotteau! *Über die Liebe*, Ortega y Gasset, p. 137.

165 Spooky impression ... their fingers. *Typoskript, ohne Titel [Amerika, 1951] (Typescript, without Title [America, 1951])* by Max Frisch, Max Frisch Archive.

167 like ... enormous length. *Toteninsel (Isle of the Dead)* by Gerhard Meier, Basel 2008, p. 26.

169 One will ... done so. *Silencing the Past: Power and the Production of History* by Michel-Rolph Trouillot, Boston 2015, p. 82.

180 Je considérais ... de Dieu. *Pérégrinations d'une paria 1833-1834 (Peregrinations of a Pariah)* by Flora Tristan, Paris 1838, p. 46.

180 J'avais ... froids, calculateurs. Ibid, p. 47.

181 You say ... and disappears. In *Das nächste Jahrhundert wird uns gehören: Frauen und Utopie 1830-1840 (The Next Century Will be Ours: Women and Utopia 1830-1840)* edited by Claudia von Alemann, Dominique Jallamion, and Bettina Schäfer, Frankfurt 1981, pp. 241-243.

183 the lust ... our pores. *Pérégrinations,* Tristan, p. 65f.

184 Il est ... la cuisine. *Oviri: Écrits d'un sauvage (Oviri: Writings of a Savage)* by Paul Gauguin, Paris 1974, p. 270.

185 Toussaint-Louverture ... a servant. *Histoire de la captivité et de la mort de Toussaint-Louverture: notre pèlerinage au fort de Joux (The History of the Captivity and Death of Toussaint-Louverture: Our Pilgrimage to Fort de Joux)* by Alfred Nemours, Paris 1929, p. 14.

188 il me ... de sucre. Ibid, p. 195.

190 The journey ... to Paris. *Briefe (Letters)* in *Sämtliche Werke: Brandenburger Ausgabe, Band IV/2 (All Works: Brandenburger Ausgabe,* Vol. IV/2) by Heinrich von Kleist and edited by Peter Staengle, Basel 1999, p. 464ff.

190 Nothing can ... ice-covered path. *Briefe,* Kleist, p. 480ff.

190 in which ... had died. Ibid, p. 483.

191 a man ... beget a child. Ibid, p. 119.

191 quite enclosed ... the city. Ibid, p. 206.

191 Use of ... overseas. *Die helvetischen Halbbrigaden im Dienste Frankreichs 1798-1805* (*The Helvetic Half Brigades in the Service of France 1798-1805*) by Fernando Bernoulli, Frauenfeld 1934, p. 94.

192 auctioned off. *The Slaves Who Defeated Napoléon: Toussaint Louverture and the Haitian War of Independence, 1801-1804* by Philippe R. Girard, Tuscaloosa 2011, p. 279.

192 That was ... my britches. *Lottokönig: Einmal Millionär und zurück* (Lotto king: Once a millionaire and back again) by Werner Bruni, Gockhausen 2010, p. 117.

197 the fifteen-cent ... countless. Ibid., p. 17.

204 I was ... could have imagined. Ibid., p. 82.

204 escaped his fate ... lucky. "Hier ist Totentanz" ("Here Is the Dance of Death") by Thomas Hüetlin in *Der Spiegel* 52/1996.

205 FOCUS: Have ... we were. "Einmal im Leben..." ("Once in a Lifetime...") by Jens Nordlohne in *FOCUS Magazine* 29/1995.

215 merchant spirit ... spoke up again. *Inkel und Yariko* (Inkel and Yariko) by Johann Jakob Bodmer, Zurich 1756.

238 a N----. *Lottokönig*, Bruni, p. 114.

240 Distribution of her relics. *Die Erziehung des Herzens* (*Sentimental Education*) by Gustave Flaubert and translated from French (*L'Éducation sentimentale*, 1869) by Emil Alfons Rheinhardt, Zurich 1979, p. 556.

DOROTHEE ELMIGER was born in 1985 in Switzerland. She is the author of *Out of the Sugar Factory*, *Shift Sleepers*, and *Invitation to the Bold of Heart*. Elmiger has been awarded numerous prizes, including the Aspekte Literature Prize for the best debut novel written in German, the 2021 Schiller Prize, and most recently the 2022 Nicolas Born Prize. *Out of the Sugar Factory* was shortlisted for both the German and the Swiss Book Award. Elmiger is an editor at Volte Books. She lives in New York City.

MEGAN EWING is a translator and Assistant Professor of German at the University of Michigan, Ann Arbor.